Lov

The Duke put ...

ing beside him, gave him hers.

"Let me tell you," the Duke said quietly, "that I think you are utterly and completely magnificent! No other woman could have been as brave or wonderful as you!"

Mimosa blushed.

They rode on in silence.

The daylight was fading fast, but she knew the Duke was eager to get her away from danger.

'I love him!' she thought. 'I love him . . . but he must never know it!'

A Camfield Novel of Love
by Barbara Cartland

———

"Barbara Cartland's novels are all distinguished by their intelligence, good sense, and good nature. . . ."
— **ROMANTIC TIMES**

"Who could give better advice on how to keep your romance going strong than the world's most famous romance novelist, Barbara Cartland?"
— **THE STAR**

Camfield Place,
Hatfield
Hertfordshire,
England

Dearest Reader,

Camfield Novels of Love mark a very exciting era of my books with Jove. They have already published nearly two hundred of my titles since they became my first publisher in America, and now all my original paperback romances in the future will be published exclusively by them.

As you already know, Camfield Place in Hertfordshire is my home, which originally existed in 1275, but was rebuilt in 1867 by the grandfather of Beatrix Potter.

It was here in this lovely house, with the best view in the county, that she wrote *The Tale of Peter Rabbit*. Mr. McGregor's garden is exactly as she described it. The door in the wall that the fat little rabbit could not squeeze underneath and the goldfish pool where the white cat sat twitching its tail are still there.

I had Camfield Place blessed when I came here in 1950 and was so happy with my husband until he died, and now with my children and grandchildren, that I know the atmosphere is filled with love and we have all been very lucky.

It is easy here to write of love and I know you will enjoy the Camfield Novels of Love. Their plots are definitely exciting and the covers very romantic. They come to you, like all my books, with love.

Bless you,

CAMFIELD NOVELS OF LOVE

by Barbara Cartland

A NEW CAMFIELD NOVEL OF LOVE BY

Barbara Cartland

Love in the Ruins

JOVE BOOKS, NEW YORK

LOVE IN THE RUINS

A Jove Book / published by arrangement with
the author

PRINTING HISTORY
Jove edition / October 1995

ISBN: 0-515-11733-1

A JOVE BOOK®
Jove Books are published by The Berkley Publishing Group,
200 Madison Avenue, New York, New York 10016.
JOVE and the "J" design are trademarks
belonging to Jove Publications, Inc.

PRINTED IN THE UNITED STATES OF AMERICA

10   9   8   7   6   5   4   3   2   1

AUTHOR'S NOTE

THUBURBO Maius in Tunisia was a Phoenician City that sided with Carthage in the final Punic War.

It was taxed but not demolished by Scipio.

The Town was chosen in 27 B.C. for one of Octavius's Colonies of Veterans.

It declined in the 3rd century, was revived in the 4th by Constantine II.

The Respublica Fenix fell victim to the Vandals and was abandoned in Byzantine times.

It was rediscovered only in 1875, and the very fine ruins which thrilled me were unearthed and re-erected only in 1912.

As I sat looking at the magnificent Temple of Mercury, with its large columns and long flight of steps, this story came into my mind.

It fell into place, as my stories always do, so that now the Temple and the Town which was once a busy hubbub of people will always live in my memory.

Love in the Ruins

chapter one

1884

MIMOSA Shenson stared at the letter in her hand, finding it impossible to believe what she read.

The small house her Father had rented in Tunis had been looked after by a Tunisian woman while they were away.

The place was clean and tidy, but Mimosa felt constricted, as if she were suddenly imprisoned.

She went to the window, and the blazing afternoon sun poured in.

It made her instantly feel too hot, and she brushed her hair away from her forehead.

She looked down at the letter in her hand and read it again.

Could it really be true?

It seemed impossible.

She looked at the date and realised it had been

written some weeks earlier.

In fact, it must have arrived immediately after she and her Father set out for Thuburbo Maius with their caravan of camels.

Her Father had been determined to incorporate an account of what had been a Roman City in his book.

However, only a little of it had been excavated so far.

They had caught the men erecting their tents on some level ground outside the area of the excavations.

It was something Mimosa had experienced at many other Roman sites.

She knew exactly how excited her Father would be by what he found, and what he knew would furnish material for his book.

It was immediately after her Mother had died nearly four years before that he had said in a harsh voice:

"If you think I can stay here missing your Mother every minute of the day and night, you are very much mistaken!"

Because she knew how much he was suffering, Mimosa answered:

"What do you want to do, Papa?"

"I am going abroad," he said. "I will write a book, which is what I have always intended to do, about the countries conquered by the Romans, and perhaps that will help me in some way to live without your Mother."

The agony in his voice was very obvious.

Mimosa had known there was nothing she could

2

do but agree with everything he suggested.

It seemed impossible that her Mother should have died so quickly and so unexpectedly.

She had contracted pneumonia during the cold Winter and had refused to take it seriously until it was too late.

Mimosa had looked around the attractive Elizabethian-built house which had been her home all her life.

She could not believe that her Father really meant to leave it for ever.

Sir Richard Shenson, however, sold it with the small Estate on which it stood, to the first person who offered to purchase it.

When they left England they took with them nothing but the clothes necessary for their journey.

It was an impulsive action that was characteristic of him.

It was the way, Mimosa knew, in which he had swept her Mother off her feet when they first met.

He had persuaded her to run away with him.

It was a romantic story that she loved hearing over and over again ever since she was a child.

She thought now that her Father would have chosen to die as he had—suddenly and unexpectedly from a snake-bite among the Roman ruins.

He would not have been happy lingering on to a slow and boring old age.

The bite of the snake was known locally to be very poisonous.

It had ensured his death after only a few hours.

It was then that Mimosa realised she would have to take charge.

The Tunisian camel-men were in such a state of consternation that they could hardly bear to touch her Father's body.

It was this attitude which had decided her not to have him taken back to Tunis.

Instead, he was buried among the ruins of Thuburbo Maius, which had so delighted him from the moment he had set eyes on them.

He had already gathered a great deal of material for his book.

They had visited when they left England, first the many Roman remains in the South of France.

From there they had sailed to Egypt, then to Libya, from where they had come to Tunis.

To Mimosa it had been a joy.

She was thrilled by the history of the way the Romans had conquered so much of the world.

She was also happy because her Father seemed a little less miserable.

Nothing, she knew, could ever compensate him for the loss of his wife.

He had adored her from the first moment he saw her.

It had been at a Ball which Mimosa's Grandfather had given at Crombe Castle for her Mother and her twin sister.

It was his son, the Viscount Crombe, who mattered more to the Earl of Crombefeld than any of his possessions.

He had, however, felt it his duty to launch his two

extremely beautiful daughters on the world in the conventional manner.

He had pooh-poohed the idea of giving a Ball for them in London.

If Society, he asserted, was interested in meeting his family, they could make the effort to come to the Castle.

It was where, in his own way, he reigned like a King.

Intolerant, arrogant, overwhelming, he expected what amounted to a feudal obedience not only from those he employed, but also from his children.

His son had escaped from his Father's domination by going first to Eton, then to Oxford.

After that he joined the Grenadier Guards, the "family Regiment."

For the girls, Lady Winifred and Lady Emily, there was no such escape.

If they wished to rebel, there was nothing they could do about it.

The Ball, Lady Winifred had told her daughter, had been a wild excitement from the first moment it was proposed.

It was to be a splendid and important occasion because the Earl knew it was expected of him.

He never did anything by halves.

Everyone in the neighbourhood was required to accommodate as many guests as could be packed into their houses.

The Castle itself was filled with the most important of the Earl's social acquaintances.

Of course there were also Gentlemen whom he con

sidered to be eligible bachelors.

From the time his daughters were old enough to be presented to the Queen, he began to consider what would be suitable marriages for them.

"But, suppose, Papa," his daughter Winifred had asked, "we do not fall in love with the men you choose to be our husbands?"

The Earl scowled at her.

"Love will come after marriage," he said. "What is your duty as my daughter is to marry somebody suitable, whose blood is as blue as ours and who can keep you in the manner to which you are accustomed."

The way he spoke made his daughter Emily, who was the more timid of the twins, shiver.

But Winifred, being braver, objected:

"I think, Papa, I would be unhappy if I had to marry a man I did not love."

"You will marry whoever I tell you to marry!" the Earl declared. "I will have none of this modern nonsense of a girl choosing her own husband when she has a Father to do it for her."

Lady Winifred did not argue.

When she fell in love with Richard Shenson, she knew that her Father would never approve of him.

He was, in fact, the best-looking and the most attractive man she had ever imagined.

He had been brought to the Ball by some neighbours who lived only a short distance from the Castle.

After he had danced three times with Lady Winifred, he persuaded her to meet him the following day.

They would not be seen in the woods which lay between the Earl's Estate and that of Richard Shenson's friends.

Richard told Lady Winifred that he had fallen in love with her from the moment he saw her.

"It may seem strange and improbable to you," he said, "but I swear to you on everything I hold sacred that you are the woman I have been looking for all my life. My only chance of being happy— really happy—is if you will marry me."

As Lady Winifred felt the same about him, she knew he was telling her the truth.

What she also knew was that her Father would not consider him for one moment as his son-in-law.

The Earl had already told her that she was to be particularly charming to the Marquess of Burford, who was the elder son of the Duke of Belminster.

Lady Winifred had danced with him.

But she had known from the moment he put his arm round her waist that she could never, even if her Father crucified her for it, accept him as her husband.

The Marquess was a squat, fat, and exceedingly plain young man with an obvious awareness of his own importance.

He spoke to her in a condescending manner which she resented.

As she told her sister, it "made her hackles rise."

As they moved over the Dance-Floor she had seen her Father talking earnestly to the Duke.

She had known by the way the eyes of the two men followed her what they were planning.

She tried to tell Richard Shenson that their love was hopeless.

But he simply put his arms round her and kissed her, and the words had died on her lips.

"I love you!" he said. "I will speak to your Father immediately."

"It will be . . . useless," Lady Winifred managed to murmur. "He will . . . never allow me to . . . marry anyone who has not . . . a title and who he . . . does not think is of . . . equal importance to . . . himself."

"I will be a Baronet when my Father dies," Richard pointed out, "but that may not be for perhaps twenty years."

Lady Winifred looked up at him with tears in her eyes.

"How can . . . this have . . . happened to . . . us?" she asked in a broken little voice.

"That we have found each other is the only thing that matters," Richard Shenson declared, "but it does mean, my darling, that you will have to be very brave."

Lady Winifred looked at him enquiringly, not understanding.

"It means," he explained quietly, "that we will have to elope. I will get a Special Licence, and once we are married there will be nothing your Father can do about it."

"He will . . . never forgive . . . me," Winifred murmured.

"Does that really matter so much?" Richard Shenson asked.

There was no need for her to answer.

They had run away.

Richard Shenson organised it so cleverly that they were married and on their way to France before the Earl was aware of what had happened.

His rage echoed round the Castle like a North wind.

He was so furious that the staff in the kitchens were trembling.

Even the dogs hid under the tables, as if they were afraid of what might happen next.

The Earl swore that he would never speak to his daughter again.

Sending for his Solicitors, he cut her out from his Will.

It was perhaps inevitable that Lady Emily should follow the lead shown by her twin sister.

They had always done everything together.

They were so much alike and so much a part of each other that they were more like one person than two.

Lady Emily kept very quiet about it and her sister's letters.

The Earl had no idea how frequently she heard from her.

Two months later she followed her sister's lead and ran away with the man with whom she in her turn had fallen in love.

This time it was an even worse blow to the Earl.

His daughter Winifred had defied him to marry

the man she loved, but at least he was an Englishman.

Lady Emily, to his horror and indignation, had chosen an American.

Clint Tison was visiting England, and at twenty-five, with a number of love-affairs behind him, had not expected to lose his heart so completely.

But he knew at once that without Lady Emily his world could never be complete as he wanted it to be.

He wooed her in a manner which left her breathless, with her heart turning somersaults.

He told her he wanted to lay the world at her feet, and that he could not live without her.

After the insipid overtures and the unimaginative compliments of her English suitors, Lady Emily found Clint Tison irresistible.

Just as her sister had, she lost her heart.

Also her will to do anything but what he told her.

They were married early one morning in the Grosvenor Chapel in South Molton Street.

By the evening they had embarked on a ship bound for New York.

This time there was nobody to listen to the Earl's raging except his son.

The Viscount hastily left the house for his Club.

Lady Emily wrote to her twin sister:

"I hope Papa will come round in time, but it is of no consequence.
"Clint is already very well off and may one day inherit a large fortune, although

none of that matters beside him. Oh, Winifred, I am so happy, just as you are, and all I want now is that you should meet Clint."

Lady Winifred was no less eager for her sister to meet her husband.

She thought Richard was the most perfect man in the world, and no-one could equal him.

It was a year before the twins saw each other again.

By that time they were both expecting babies.

They felt it was the most exciting thing that had ever happened to them.

Because Richard and Clint wanted their wives to be happy, they bought houses which were near each other's.

Clint's business interests were in America.

This meant he would not live in his attractive English Georgian Manor much of the time.

But they came to England nearly every year.

Clint had made one stipulation before his marriage.

That was that his wife would not use her courtesy title.

He felt, if the Earl would not accept his son-in-law, his marriage had nothing to do with the English.

"You will be Mrs. Tison," he said to Lady Emily.

"That is all I want to be, darling," she answered truthfully.

As Winifred's and Emily's daughters were born

within a month of each other, they were as close as if they too were twins.

Because Clint found it difficult to be away from America for long, there were sometimes intervals of more than a year before Mimosa could meet her Cousin Minerva again.

She had, in fact, not seen her for a year when Lady Winifred died so unexpectedly.

Mimosa had written to Minerva to tell her what had occurred, and also to say that she was going abroad with her Father.

She told her that since he had sold the house she had no idea what would happen when they returned.

She was nearly eighteen and had been making plans with her Father and Mother.

They had decided that after she had been presented at Court they would give a Ball for her.

This was to take place in April.

But by the time that month arrived, Mimosa had already gone abroad with her Father.

Now, nearly four years later, Mimosa's thoughts were on Minerva.

She knew there was no-one else to whom she could turn in the crisis which had so unexpectedly overtaken her.

She looked down at the Solicitor's letter in her hand.

Could it be possible—really possible—that what he had written was the truth?

When she and her Father had left England, he had instructed his Solicitors to send money to every country they visited.

There had been money transferred for them in Banks everywhere.

Mimosa knew her Father had not worried about the cost of anything they bought, as long as it was helpful for his purposes.

When they were not sleeping in tents on some ancient Roman site, they stayed at the best Hotel in the vicinity.

If he did not think it comfortable enough, he rented a house for a month or so.

There he would write his accounts of what he had seen.

Mimosa would then copy them out in her clear, attractive hand-writing.

They would then be legible when there was a chance of their going to print.

The most precious possession they carried on their travels was the material of her Father's book.

It seemed to Mimosa he had so much to say that it would run into several volumes.

Because they were moving about without any fixed address, it was difficult to receive letters.

However, before they had left Libya for Tunis, he had written to his Solicitors.

He instructed them to send money to a Tunis Bank.

Because he had been in a hurry to visit Thuburbo Maius, he had not gone to the Bank himself.

Instead, he sent a message by one of the native servants to have money available for them on their return.

Thuburbo Maius was only fifty miles from Tunis.

Because Sir Richard thought it would make one of the most exciting chapters in his book, he could not wait to get there.

It had, in fact, been discovered, or, rather, the Archaeological World had become aware of it, in 1873.

It had not at the time caused the sensation it might have.

So many other things were happening in Tunisia.

The suppression of piracy had left a substantial deficit in the Bey of Tunis's treasury.

This meant that the economic condition of the whole country had seriously deteriorated.

In their wretchedness the people revolted.

For this they suffered fierce measures of repression, and bloody fighting resulted in a triumph for the Bey's troops.

The economy deteriorated even further owing to several years of drought and subsequent famine.

Finally the Bey's Prime Minister, the man chiefly responsible for the country's ruin, was removed.

Tunisia was bankrupt and prey to the covetous ambitions of the Colonial Powers.

Sir Richard and Mimosa were at that time in Algeria.

They were not, therefore, surprised at what they learnt.

The French, following a disturbance on the border between Algeria and Tunisia, decided to invade the latter troubled country.

The Bey's Army offered little resistance.

In May 1881 the Bey signed a Treaty accepting that Tunisia became a Protectorate of France.

To Sir Richard Shenson it was good news.

It meant that, under the French, order would be restored and it would be possible for him to visit, as he was longing to do, Carthage, El Djem, Thuburbo Maius, and other Roman remains.

They had arrived in Tunis three years later, in 1884, to find, as Sir Richard anticipated, everything apparently under control.

A great number of the people were already speaking French.

The Tunisians smiled a welcome at every visitor, knowing it would mean money in their pockets.

But now, after waiting for so long for what he thought would be an Archaeologist's or a Historian's El Dorado, Sir Richard was dead.

Mimosa was confronted with a letter from the Solicitors in London, informing them that there was no money left.

She found it impossible to believe this was the truth.

But unfortunately the fact was that the Company in which Sir Richard had unwisely invested all his capital had gone bankrupt.

Her Father had been buried in an unidentified grave.

She had no friend to whom she could turn for advice.

It was frightening to know she was penniless.

She had paid off the camel-drivers who had taken them to Thuburbo Maius with the cash her Father had had with him.

She had tipped them generously, as he had always done.

She thought as she had returned to Tunis without him that now she would have to go back to England.

That in itself was a frightening prospect.

She was not certain where she would be welcome.

As far as she knew, her Father and Mother were so completely happy with each other that they had never kept in touch with any of their relatives.

With the exception of her Aunt Emily and Cousin Minerva, Mimosa knew no-one in England.

It was now nearly four years since she had been there.

It seemed extraordinary that at the age of twenty-one she had no English friends, no-one to whom she could turn in an emergency.

What was still more frightening, she did not have any money.

How could she get back to her own country?

It suddenly seemed to her as if the world had fallen in ruins about her.

She might be standing in a Thuburbo Maius of her own with nothing but rubble round her feet and no roof over her head.

"I am suffering from shock," Mimosa told herself sensibly. "I am sure I shall be able to think more clearly in a little while."

At the moment, however, there was no sunshine outside shedding its golden haze over everything.

Instead, even the white buildings which she thought so beautiful seemed dark.

She was not crying only because she had lost her Father.

She was crying for herself, left in a hostile, terrifying world where she was completely alone.

"What shall . . . I do?" she asked. "Oh . . . God . . . tell me what . . . to do."

It was a prayer that came from the very depths of her heart.

For the moment there appeared to be no answer.

There was only the letter in her hand which told her she had no money.

She was still standing at the window when the door of the room opened.

The old woman who had looked after the house while they were away came in.

She was carrying a cup in which, Mimosa knew, there would be mint tea.

She took it from her and sipped the warm, sweet liquid.

In this part of the world it was a remedy for every trouble and every worry.

The old woman picked up the envelope which had contained the letter and put it tidily on the table.

She had brought in a newspaper which she also set down on the table.

Mimosa knew it was the newspaper which her Father had ordered as soon as they reached Tunis.

It was a French paper and had been put into publication as soon as the French had occupied the country.

Whcrever they went, the French introduced their own newspapers.

All Frenchmen living abroad wanted news of their beloved France, and, of course, the gaieties of Paris.

Miserable and upset though she was, Mimosa thought it was kind of the old woman to have remembered her Father's wishes.

Then, insidiously, the question came into her mind as to how she would be able to pay for it.

More important still, how was she to pay the old woman's wages.

She was sure, or thought she was, that her Father had paid the rent for several months.

It was the House Agent who had found them somebody to look after them.

The old woman had a son whom Mimosa remembered her Father also paid.

She thought the servants would not have been given money for much more than the weeks he would be away.

He would probably have paid them up to the week after he expected to return.

She worked it out in her mind.

This would give her a few days in which to discover how she could live and pay for the food she would need.

But how was she to find enough money to pay for her return to England?

She supposed, although she was not sure, that there was a British Consulate of some sort in Tunis.

She imagined that if she explained to them her predicament and who she was, they would be willing to help her.

At the same time, it was terrifying to know that

even when she reached England, there would be no money waiting for her.

Nor would there be any home to go to.

Too late, she wondered why she had not begged her Father not to sell the house so that, if he did not wish to return to it, she would be able to do so.

But he had been in such a hurry to get away because he was so desperately unhappy at her Mother's death.

It was for this reason that she had not questioned anything he had arranged.

"What . . . am I . . . to do? Oh . . . God . . . what am . . . I to . . . do?" she asked again as she drank the warm tea.

It then struck her that perhaps she would be wise to stay in Tunis and try to find some sort of employment.

Fortunately she could speak a number of languages.

Her Mother had been insistent that she should be proficient in French.

That was the language she needed at the moment.

Because her Father was multi-lingual, she was also able to speak Italian and, more important still, Arabic.

She thought perhaps there would be children whose parents wanted them to learn languages.

It was certainly an idea.

As she was trying to follow the twists and turns of her mind, she picked up the newspaper.

As she expected, the first few pages gave the news in French of what was happening in France. There was nothing about England on the first three pages.

She turned to the advertisements, wondering if by chance there was anybody advertising for a Teacher.

Any situation, even a very humble one, would be better than having to explain her predicament to the English Consul, if there was one.

She turned over two more pages, then saw there was an item headed:

EVENTS IN TUNIS

There was one paragraph about a disturbance which had taken place in the centre of the Town. Reading on, Mimosa saw below it:

TRAGEDY IN SIDI BOU SAID

Almost without realising she was doing so, she read:

> "It is with deep regret and anxiety that we report that it is now over two months since the disappearance of Mademoiselle Minerva Tison.
>
> "It is locally believed that she was kidnapped from her home, Villa l'Astre Bleu, by gangsters who have been causing a great deal of trouble and distress in Tunis recently.
>
> "The Authorities have been waiting to hear what ransom is required for Mademoiselle Tison, who is known to be very

rich, but no demand has come.

"The Authorities and those concerned with her disappearance fear she may have lost her life in an effort to escape, and the story will never have an ending.

"Mademoiselle Tison was well known on the hill of Sidi Bou Said, where she had bought a Villa. It is a little way below the famous shrine which pilgrims and tourists from the City visit in increasing numbers.

"The Corsairs made Sidi Bou Said the mascot of their Patron Saint of Anti-Christian Piracy. But it seems that even today, when the Corsairs have gone, piracy can still take place on this famous site."

Mimosa read, then re-read the paragraph.

At first her heart had leapt to think that miraculously Minerva was so near her.

Then as she realised she was missing, perhaps dead, she felt her whole being cry out at the horror of it.

She had lost her Mother and her Father, and now her Cousin Minerva, who was almost a twin sister to her.

"It is . . . cruel! It is . . . wicked!" she raged against the fates.

Then suddenly it was as if in answer to her prayer, God was speaking to her.

She knew what she must do.

21

chapter two

WHEN the old woman came in in the morning, Mimosa was already up and dressed.

She was wearing a cape over her gown and had a chiffon scarf to put over her head rather than a hat.

The woman looked at her in surprise, thinking how early she was.

Mimosa was ready with what she had decided to tell her.

"My friends are taking me to England today," she said slowly in Tunisian, "and I have therefore no time to go to the Bank and obtain money with which to reward you for your services."

She thought the old woman looked at her apprehensively, and continued:

"As I cannot stay to pack my clothes and my Father's, I am giving them to you."

23

She saw the woman look at her in astonishment, and went on:

"I am sure some of the clothes my Father wore will fit your son, and the rest will realise quite a lot of money if you sell them."

She knew this was true, because among her Father's things was a fur-lined coat which he wore when it was cold.

With a lofty air she said:

"I have also no wish to take with me the clothes I have been wearing for some time and which are now out of date, but I am sure you will find a purchaser for them and they are in good condition."

She paused before she added slowly:

"There is only one thing I would ask of you— that you will be kind enough to get your son, or someone, to take to the Villa *l'Astre Bleu* at Sidi Bou Said the parcel which I have put on the table."

She indicated it with her hand.

It was a large parcel because it contained all the pages her Father had written for his book.

She knew it was the one thing she could not leave behind or lose.

The only way she could be certain it would be safe was if it went to the Villa addressed to Minerva.

The woman nodded to show she understood, and Mimosa said:

"Thank you very much for all you have done, and I know you will return the key of the house to the agent who let it to us, and engaged you to look after it."

She held out her hand and the woman clasped it then kissed it.

The gesture told Mimosa that she was thrilled with what she had been offered and would not miss the actual money which she was unable to give her.

Mimosa then wrapped the chiffon scarf round her neck and over her hair and walked out of the house.

She knew the woman, intent on seeing what she had been left in the way of clothes, would be too interested in them to notice where she went.

She would not notice either if there were people waiting to escort her to the ship which was to take her to England.

Mimosa walked away, thinking that it was becoming a habit in her family to walk out of their houses leaving everything they possessed behind.

She was only thankful that she had remembered that, while she had abandoned everything else, she must keep her Father's book.

He had rid himself of everything that had belonged to her Mother.

Mimosa could not help remembering what a terrible waste it had seemed when, on the ship that carried them away from their own country, he had disposed of her Mother's jewels.

She had seen him coming from his cabin carrying what she recognised as her Mother's jewel-case.

Everything else that had belonged to her Mother had been left behind in the house.

She supposed that the man who had bought it would dispose of her Mother's gowns and anything else she had possessed.

Worrying over her Father's distress, she had not thought of the jewellery.

Then, when she saw the jewel-case in his hands, she was surprised that he had brought it with him.

"What are you doing with that, Papa?" she had asked.

Her Father looked at her with the agony in his eyes that had been there ever since his wife's death.

"I will not allow anyone, not even you," he replied, "to wear the jewels I gave to your Mother with love, and because she meant everything to me. They will lie at the bottom of the sea, and will be a tombstone to her beauty."

He walked away as he spoke, and Mimosa had been too stunned to follow him.

She knew when he came back to his cabin that he had thrown the jewel-case into the sea and it would never be seen again.

It was the impetuous, dashing, idealistic way he had always behaved.

She knew that his book, which meant so much to him, was also idealistic in a way which would help and inspire those who read it.

Fortunately the house which they had rented in Tunis was on the outskirts of the Town, leading towards Sidi Bou Said.

However, it was still a long walk.

By the time Mimosa reached the hill which led up to the shrine, she was beginning to feel exhausted.

At first there had been few people in the streets. Now there were more.

26

The traffic and the crowds were increasing so that people would not notice her or question why she was alone.

She started to climb the steep hill which led up to the shrine. There were just a few Villas at the base of it.

Then there was an occasional one on the way up.

They obviously belonged to rich people, because the Villas themselves were large and spotlessly maintained.

The gardens were filled with flowers and trees.

They were enclosed by walls to ensure privacy.

The scent of jasmine filled the air.

Mimosa knew that many people who climbed to the shrine thought of it as a charm that could protect them from the "Evil Eye."

The Tunisians were very superstitious and carried Nigella seeds in their pockets.

The majority of them hid a charm in their clothes or in the gold lockets which the women wore round their necks.

The symbolism of the charms dated back to the beginning of time.

The hand of Fatima was, she knew, one of the most favoured.

She wished now, as she climbed slowly up the hill, that she had one herself.

No-one needed luck more than she did at this particular moment.

She could feel the beating of her heart, not only from the physical exertion but also because she was afraid.

Then she told herself that if Minerva turned up, everything would be all right.

If she did not, then at least she had a chance of saving herself.

Mimosa prayed that God would help her.

She hoped this would not clash with the religion which brought pilgrims to the shrine at the top of the hill.

She remembered the Moslem legend that the famous St. Louis did not die on Byrsa Hill.

He took leave of his Army, married a Berber girl, and became the local Saint Bou Said.

He was known for curing rheumatism and for stopping scorpions from stinging.

On their travels, Sir Richard and Mimosa had discovered so many strange faiths and beliefs.

She only wished now she could talk to her Father about Sidi Bou Said.

At last, when she had almost reached the top, she saw in front of her a large, white, and very beautiful Villa.

She knew without being told that this was *l'Astre Bleu* and there was no need to look for the name on the gate.

She paused for a moment.

Then, looking up at the sky, she prayed fervently that she would be successful in what she was undertaking.

There were some large bushes outside the gate.

She took off her cape which had made her very hot.

She pushed it into the bushes until it was impossible to see it.

Anybody who saw her now would be aware that her gown was dusty, dirty, and torn in several places.

She had chosen one of the oldest gowns she possessed, which she had worn for at least two years.

It had taken some time to roll it in the dust and add water to make mud with which the skirt was splattered.

By the time she had finished, it looked very disreputable.

She pulled off the scarf which had covered her hair and hid that too in the bushes.

It was unlikely, she thought, that anyone would find it and her cape.

If they did, they would assume it had been dropped by some pilgrim feeling exhausted after the climb up the hill.

She opened the gate and walked in.

The flowers in the garden were breathtakingly beautiful.

The birds were singing in the trees.

Mimosa thought it was like stepping into a Heaven of peace where there were no problems and no fear.

She followed a tiled path towards a door.

It was fronted by a portico which had a number of white pillars to support it.

The door was open.

As she wondered whether she should walk in, a woman appeared.

She was carrying a basket on her arm as if she were going into the garden to pick flowers.

She was a middle-aged woman with dark eyes.

As Mimosa had hoped she would, she gave a thrill cry, threw her basket down on the ground, and exclaimed in French:

"Mademoiselle! Mademoiselle! You have returned!"

Her voice rose as she went on:

"You have come home! But where have you been? We have been looking for you everywhere, trying frantically to find you!"

She moved forward as she spoke, and reaching Mimosa, put her arms round her.

Mimosa just stared at her blankly.

"Who . . . who am I . . . and . . . why am I . . . here?"

The woman stared at her.

"You are home! We have missed you. We thought you had been kidnapped. Oh, *Mademoiselle,* thank *le Bon Dieu* that you have come back to us!"

There was a hint of tears in the woman's voice, but Mimosa only said dully:

"Where . . . am I? I . . . I cannot . . . remember."

The woman took her by the arm.

"Come inside," she said. "What have they done to you, those devils? Oh, my poor *Mademoiselle,* have they hurt you?"

Mimosa allowed herself to be led into a large, beautifully furnished Sitting-Room.

Its long windows opened out into the garden.

The Frenchwoman sat her down in a chair, saying:

"You are hot and tired! I will get you something to drink."

She hurried from the room.

Mimosa could hear her calling out that *Mademoiselle* was back and giving orders for food and drink.

Then she came back and, kneeling by the chair in which Mimosa was sitting, she said:

"Just rest, then you will feel better."

"I . . . I cannot . . . remember . . ." Mimosa murmured. "Who . . . am . . . I?"

"You are Minerva Tison," the Frenchwoman said slowly and clearly. "Minerva Tison—that is your name."

Mimosa did not repeat it, she merely looked blankly at the Frenchwoman.

"I am Suzette. Surely you remember me? Suzette, whom you used to laugh with and say she was your right-hand."

"Su . . . ze . . . tte," Mimosa said slowly, hesitating over both syllables.

"That is right," the Frenchwoman said, "and you are Minerva."

Mimosa shut her eyes for a moment.

Suzette rose to her feet as a servant came in with a tray on which there was coffee and some *petits-fours*.

Suzette poured out the coffee and gave it to Mimosa.

She took it from her tentatively.

Then she sipped a little of it, feeling it was what she needed after walking so far, and Suzette asked gently:

"Can you remember what happened to you after you were taken away?"

Mimosa shook her head from side to side.

"I . . . I can . . . remember . . . nothing . . . who I am . . . or why I am . . . here."

"Then they must have beaten you," Suzette said angrily. "Those wicked, wicked men! If only we could catch them. They would be punished for the way they have treated you!"

Then, deciding it was the sensible thing to do, she said:

"I think, *Mademoiselle,* you should go upstairs and sleep. I am sure you will wake up remembering what has happened and knowing who you are."

She thought Mimosa looked as if she did not understand and helped her out of the chair.

With Suzette supporting her, she went slowly up the stairs.

There was a wide landing, then what Mimosa thought was the most beautiful bedroom she had ever seen.

There was a huge bed with the headboard in the shape of a silver shell.

The bed-cover was made of exquisite lace which must have cost a fortune.

All the furniture was inlaid with mother-of-pearl.

A looking glass on the dressing-table was surrounded by angels painted in their natural colour.

Suzette found Mimosa an exquisitely beautiful

nightgown which she thought could have come only from Paris.

It must have been worked by Nuns.

She remembered how Minerva had told her she had bought a *négligée* in France when she was there with her Mother.

Suzette helped Mimosa into bed, and when she was lying back against the pillows, she hurried away.

Mimosa was certain it was to send messages to the French Authorities who had been looking for Minerva, to announce that she had arrived home.

She drew a deep breath of thankfulness.

So far Suzette had not queried for a moment that she was not who she pretended to be.

After all, there was no reason why anyone in Tunis should have the slightest idea that Minerva Tison had a Cousin who looked exactly like her.

Yet now, when she could think about it quietly, it seemed extraordinary that Minerva should have been living alone in the Villa without her Father or Mother, or, in fact, with only this Frenchwoman who, she supposed, was a paid employee.

"What can have happened to Aunt Emily?" Mimosa wondered.

She had always found Clint Tison charming and he had certainly been very kind to her.

The whole thing was most mysterious, and she longed to ask a thousand questions.

But she knew she had to play her part carefully, and it might be a long time before she could find the answers she longed to hear.

Because she had not slept well the previous night, she actually dozed for a little while.

She woke when Suzette came hurrying into the room to say unnecessarily:

"Are you awake, *Mademoiselle*? *Monsieur* Beaton, who has been investigating your disappearance, is here and wants to talk to you."

Mimosa opened her eyes wide.

"Where . . . am . . . I?" she asked. "I . . . I do not know . . . who I . . . am."

"I told you that you are Minerva Tison," Suzette answered. "But do not worry, just let *Monsieur* talk to you for a few minutes. I will explain to him that you are very tired and it may take time before your memory returns."

Suzette went from the room and Mimosa could hear her say outside the door:

"She still does not know who she is. I think those ghastly men must have hit her on the head, or perhaps treated her so badly that she has been unconscious."

"At least she is home!" a man with a deep voice replied. "And that, *Madame,* is all that matters."

"Of course, of course," Suzette agreed.

She opened the door wider to say:

"Here, *Mademoiselle,* is *Monsieur* Beaton."

Mimosa turned her head.

A middle-aged man was approaching her who she guessed was in charge of the Secret Police.

They were employed by the French in all the countries they occupied.

He reached the bed, and as Mimosa put out her

hand, he bent over it in a perfunctory manner without actually kissing it.

That, she knew, meant he respected her as someone of importance.

The French did not usually kiss the hands of young women, only those who were married.

As Minerva was very rich, she would be treated with the utmost respect, regardless of whether she had a husband or not.

"May I say, *Mademoiselle,*" the Frenchman began, "how delighted I am that you have returned home and were not, as we feared, murdered by those who kidnapped you, leaving no clue as to where they had taken you."

"I . . . I do not . . . remember," Mimosa said weakly.

"It will all come back to you in time," *Monsieur* Beaton said politely, "and I know how delighted everybody will be at your return."

Mimosa just inclined her head, as if to speak were too much of an effort.

There was a pause before *Monsieur* Beaton asked:

"You have no idea, I suppose, of where you have been, or who has been keeping you prisoner?"

"I . . . c-cannot . . . remember," Mimosa said again.

She saw the disappointment on the Frenchman's face, and after a moment she asked:

"Is . . . this my . . . home?"

"This is your Villa, *Mademoiselle,* and you have been living here for over a year."

"All . . . mine!" Mimosa whispered.

"*Oui,* all yours," *Monsieur* Beaton said impressively, "and *Madame* Blanc has kept it in perfect order for you. She was always convinced that somehow or other you would come back, and she never lost hope."

Mimosa registered that Suzette's surname was Blanc, and wished she could ask more, but thought it would be a mistake.

Instead, she closed her eyes as if she were tired and *Monsieur* Beaton rose to his feet.

"I will come back another day," he said. "In the meantime, once again, *Mademoiselle,* I must say how happy we all are to have you back with us."

He smiled at her and then went on:

"I promise that in future you will be well guarded, so that this sort of thing will never happen again."

Mimosa murmured a weak "thank you," and he went from the room.

She could hear him and Suzette talking animatedly as they went down the stairs.

She had won!

She had established herself as Minerva.

Monsieur Beaton had not suspected either that she was an impostor.

Because it was such a relief, she wanted to jump up and look round the Villa.

She also wanted to find out as much as she could about her Cousin.

She knew, however, that that would be unwise, and she forced herself to lie quietly in bed.

Later she ate a little of the delicious luncheon that was brought to her.

Suzette sat chatting to her while she did so.

"You must eat everything you can," she said, "or the Chef will be very disappointed."

Mimosa registered the fact that she had a Chef.

"He has been in despair while you have been away," Suzette continued, "with no-one to enjoy his soufflés, his pâtés, and all your favourite dishes. And, of course, he missed *Monsieur le Comte,* as we all did."

Mimosa stiffened.

Then she asked in a childlike little voice:

"Monsieur ... le Comte? Who is ... *Monsieur le ... Comte?"*

"Now, *Mademoiselle,* surely you must remember him? We thought at first that you were so unhappy at his departure that you had thrown yourself into the sea."

She paused, but Mimosa did not speak, so she went on:

"Then one of the gardeners said he had seen two men carrying you away and, when we found your bracelet on the path, we knew you had been kidnapped."

"Kidnapped ..." Mimosa said slowly. "I ... was kidnapped!"

"Yes, *Mademoiselle,* and it must have been terrible for you. They must have made you sleep on the floor, or perhaps ..."

She stopped as if she thought it would be a mistake to suggest that any indignities or cruelties had taken place.

Instead, she said:

"At least you have forgotten your unhappiness over *Monsieur le Comte*."

"Why . . . was I . . . unhappy?" Mimosa asked.

"Because he had to go back to France," Suzette replied. "It was terrible for you, and we were all very sorry. We all lost our hearts to him, but I expect his wife insisted on his return."

She gave a little sniff of indignation before she said:

"Women are all the same, and they can be very cruel when something affects their hearts."

Mimosa did not answer.

She thought it sounded as if her Cousin had been infatuated with this *Monsieur le Comte*, whoever he was.

Although it seemed impossible, she must have been living with him here.

And he was a married man!

How could Minerva do anything so wrong, so wicked? she wondered.

Then she asked herself whether, if she had fallen in love with a man as her Mother had, she would have been able to resist eloping with him, whether he had a wife or not.

It all seemed so improbable and difficult to understand.

She could only listen to Suzette.

She was obviously a chatter-box who had found it boring to be alone with no-one to talk to.

"Of course you were miserable and upset," Suzette went on, "and we were all so sorry for you. But because you are so lovely we were quite certain somebody else would come along."

She paused a moment and then continued:

"After all, it is very easy to fall in love in such beautiful surroundings as here at *l'Astre Bleu*."

"But . . . why are . . . you here?" Mimosa asked, hoping she did not sound too eager to know the answer.

"I am here because *Monsieur le Comte* asked me to come with you when you both left Paris. He wanted somebody sensible like myself to look after you."

"Paris!" Mimosa exclaimed, fastening on the one word. "Where is . . . Paris?"

"It is the Capital of France!" Suzette replied. "You must remember that. You were there with your Father and Mother when they were killed in that tragic train crash."

Mimosa shut her eyes.

So that was what had happened to Aunt Emily and Clint—a train crash!

Now the story was beginning to unfold before her eyes.

Minerva had been alone and the *Comte* had swept her away to where she could forget her unhappiness.

He had brought her to Tunis.

She had the idea that he might in some way be connected with the administration of Tunis under the French.

Then he had been recalled to France because his

wife, being jealous, had put pressure on the Authorities.

Trying to avoid asking too intelligent questions, Mimosa said after what seemed a long silence:

"The . . . *Comte* . . . who is the *Comte*?"

"Now you are beginning to remember him," Suzette said with satisfaction. "You called him André, but he is *le Comte* de Boussens. Surely you remember him? He was so handsome, so charming, and always laughing. *Tiens,* but I miss his laughter as much as you must have done."

Mimosa shut her eyes again, and Suzette said:

"I do not want to tire you, but if we talk about things *Monsieur* Beaton is certain your memory will come back."

She smiled before continuing:

"He told me before he left that he had had another case where a man was so cruelly beaten up by the ruffians who assaulted him that it was a month before he could think clearly, or even remember his name."

Mimosa did not answer, and after a moment Suzette said:

"Think of André, think of how happy you were together, and how much he made you laugh."

Mimosa did not speak.

She merely lay with her eyes shut, and after a moment Suzette went on as if speaking to herself:

"You poor little thing! You have been through so much! You lost your parents in that terrible rail disaster, you lost your *Cher Ami,* and they say there is no chance of his coming back."

She sniffed before she said:

"You have suffered at the hands of the kidnappers, who perhaps we shall never bring to justice. It is not fair! It is wicked that one small person should suffer so much!"

She gave an involuntary little sob, then, as if to hide her feelings, went from the room.

Mimosa opened her eyes.

She was certainly learning some strange things about her Cousin.

At the same time, she thought how awful it must have been for Minerva when her Father and Mother had been killed and she had been left all alone in Paris.

It was just as she was, alone without her Mother or Father.

The difference was that Minerva was very rich.

She owned this beautiful Villa and, if her Father was dead, his great fortune.

Mimosa knew that Clint Tison had become, during the past years, very, very rich.

She had known long ago that he had discovered oil on his land in Texas.

Because it had made no difference to her affection for Minerva, she had not really thought about it.

Nor had she realised that it could bring not only pleasure but also danger.

Of course it had been impossible for the tales of Minerva's fortune not to precede her to Tunis.

There were criminals everywhere, willing for payment to abduct or kidnap rich men and women, and even children.

41

Their employers could then extort a huge ransom for their release.

Mimosa could only fear that what the French assumed was true.

Minerva, instead of just being held for ransom, had been killed, perhaps inadvertently.

Otherwise they would have demanded ransom in the usual way.

It would have been better to pay it rather than let her suffer at the cruel hands of those who had abducted her.

Whatever the explanation, Mimosa knew that Minerva's coming to Tunis had rescued her from being penniless in a strange country.

She would otherwise have found it exceedingly difficult to return to England.

She knew when her Father died that the only people who would really welcome her in their home, and with whom she could live happily, would have been Minerva's Father and Mother.

She had thought, at first, it would be difficult to find them if they had gone back to America.

But at least their house in England would be available.

She would have been able to stay there as a guest until she could communicate with them and tell them what had happened to her Father.

Now everything was topsy-turvy.

She had insinuated herself into Minerva's place.

Now she must work out what she should do next.

She wondered how long it would be possible to go on pretending to be her Cousin.

Because it all seemed so improbable and at the same time frightening, Mimosa shrank from making decisions.

She felt it would be best, at least for the time being, to stay where she was.

It was important she should find out a little more about her Cousin's secret life.

Despite every effort not to feel shocked, she was shocked.

That Minerva should have been living in Tunis with the *Comte,* who was a married man, was to her very shocking.

Ever since they had been aware that there was something called "Love," they had talked about it together.

They had been certain there would be somebody handsome and charming, like their Fathers, who would come along and sweep them off their feet.

Then they would be as happy and content as their Mothers were.

"Can you imagine what it would be like," Mimosa remembered saying, "if your Papa and mine were like Grandpapa, determined to marry us off to some stuffy aristocrat simply because he had a title?"

"I would rather die," Mimosa had declared, "than let anyone I did not love touch me."

Mimosa had paused before she went on:

"Mama said she was terrified of Grandpapa when she was our age, and if Papa had not taken her away, she would eventually have had to marry whoever Grandpapa chose for her."

"Mama said the same thing to me," Minerva answered. "I would have refused—I know I would have refused!"

"We are very, very lucky," Mimosa said, "because neither your parents nor mine would ever make us marry somebody we did not love."

"I know that," Minerva agreed. "I am sure I shall marry a 'Prince Charming,' who I will know is the right person for me the first moment I see him."

They had both laughed at the idea.

Now it seemed to Mimosa tragic that Minerva's "Prince Charming" had turned out to be the *Comte* André, who already had a wife.

He might also have a family, Mimosa thought.

"It was wrong and wicked of him to ask Minerva to go away with him," she told herself sternly.

She also thought in her heart that it was wrong of Minerva to have listened to him.

chapter three

MIMOSA was sitting in the garden, feeling the flowers soothed and comforted her.

More than that, she thought they told her that she had done the right thing.

There was nothing so very wrong in pretending to be her Cousin.

There was no doubt that everybody had accepted her without question.

She found that Minerva had certainly made herself comfortable.

There was an excellent Chef who provided the most delicious meals, and a boy to help him in the kitchen.

There were two *femmes-de-chambre,* middle-aged women who appeared to be cleaning and polishing every minute of the day.

There was a Butler who was able also to drive the carriage if it was wanted.

Besides the servants in the house, *Monsieur* Beaton had placed two guards on duty at night and one in the daytime.

Anyone who came to the gates was interrogated.

No-one could go to the house without being authorised by them.

It appeared to Mimosa to be "shutting the stable-door after the horse had bolted."

Whoever had spirited Minerva away had never been heard of again, and neither had she.

Sometimes Mimosa felt guilty when she moved about the beautifully furnished house and thought of what Minerva had suffered or was still suffering.

She could not help feeling that, as they had heard nothing from the kidnappers, Minerva must be dead.

She had learned a great deal about her Cousin from Suzette Blanc, who was an inveterate gossip.

She had been cooped up in the Villa with nobody to talk to for so long that she now could not stop talking.

And Mimosa was willing to listen.

The more Mimosa heard, the more she was able to put together a picture of Minerva's recent life.

It was not, she knew, anything of which her Mother would have approved.

According to Suzette, the *Comte* had been the most fascinating and alluring man who had ever existed.

She eulogised about him.

She repeated to herself over and over again as she described his charm, his good manners, his various attractions.

Mimosa felt she could almost see him standing in front of her.

It surprised her that there were no pictures of him in the Villa.

She could understand, however, that, as he was apparently a married man, he had tried to keep his liaison with Minerva as secret as possible.

It was something she could not ask, but she thought perhaps he had deliberately returned to Paris because he was no longer interested in her Cousin.

It was a complicated story.

She found it difficult to fit everything Suzette said into a coherent pattern.

Now she was considering how soon she could suggest going back to England.

She had been at the Villa for nearly a week.

On the third day after her arrival the Manager of the Bank in Tunis had called to see her.

She knew that Suzette Blanc had told him that her memory had still not returned and that she was in a weak state.

He had insisted on seeing her alone.

Mimosa suspected, however, that Suzette was listening at the key-hole.

"I know that you have been through a terrible ordeal, *Mademoiselle*," he said politely, "but I am afraid I must ask you now that you have returned, to allow me to inform your Bank in London that you are able to sign cheques, so that we can put the position right where your money is concerned.''

Mimosa was listening attentively, and he went on:

''As soon as we knew you were missing, I communicated with your Bank and asked them to agree that, until you returned or the Police learnt what had happened to you, I could continue to pay the Staff here and, of course, *Madame* Blanc.''

Mimosa noted that as she had expected, Suzette Blanc was an employee, not just a friend of the *Comte*'s who had been invited to chaperon her Cousin.

''I am sure . . . I can . . . sign cheques,'' she said slowly, ''but . . . I am still . . . rather feeble.''

The Bank Manager produced a number of forms which she signed laboriously.

She knew, of course, exactly what her Cousin's signature looked like.

But to make her story more convincing, she wrote her name slowly in a large, rather childlike handwriting.

The Bank Manager seemed to be satisfied.

He asked her if she wished him to continue to pay the servants' wages and if she required any ready money.

''I have brought you,'' he said, ''what is approximately, in Tunisian money, twenty-five pounds. But, of course, *Mademoiselle*, if you require any more, you have only to send a servant with your signed cheque and it will be cashed immediately.''

"Thank you . . . thank you . . . very much," Mimosa said.

She would have liked to question him about Minerva's finances, but thought it would be a mistake.

She was sure that since her Father and Mother were both dead, at least most of their large fortune must have come to her.

Now, relaxing in the garden, she wondered how long she could keep up her pretence of being her Cousin.

Was it possible for her to continue for the rest of her life to draw on Minerva's huge fortune?

There might have been a number of other people who had benefitted under Clint Tison's Will besides his daughter.

She thought she would have to go back to England before she could see the Will or even learn the terms of it.

However, being still frightened by the whole situation, she thought the less she communicated with England until she felt brave enough to go there, the better.

There was still the biggest problem of all—how and where she was to live once she got there.

Her life had centred completely around her Father and Mother, and apart from them there had been only her Aunt Emily and Clint Tison.

And, of course, Minerva.

There had been other relatives, but the older ones had all sided with her Grandfather in condemning her Mother for running away.

The same had applied to her Aunt Emily in her turn.

"What shall I do?"

It was the same question over and over again, only now there was no hurry.

She was being well looked after.

She was safe, and what could be more comfortable than the Villa and this exquisitely beautiful garden?

She had discovered there were three gardeners to look after it.

She was thinking that the sun was growing hot and she would go under the porch.

There was a sunshade on a stand beside her.

It shaded her from the direct rays of the sun which had now risen well up a cloudless sky.

Suddenly she was aware that Suzette was beside her and looking agitated.

"*Mademoiselle,*" she said in a voice hardly above a whisper, "*Monsieur* Charlot is here to see you."

Before Mimosa could ask who he was, Suzette glanced over her shoulder and said in a voice Mimosa could hardly hear:

"Be careful of him! He is dangerous, very dangerous!"

Mimosa felt alarmed.

"Why?" she asked. "Why . . . is he . . . dangerous?"

Her brain was racing, asking who this man was.

Why was he dangerous?

Was it she or her Cousin who should be afraid of him?

Suzette did not say any more.

Mimosa was aware that the man in question had followed Suzette from the Villa and was standing beside her chair.

One glance at him told her that he was French and what her Father would have called a "Gentleman."

At the same time, there was something about him which made her feel that she must be on her guard.

Without speaking, he drew up a garden-chair that was not far from the one in which she was reclining.

He set it at her side.

Then he glanced at Suzette and said in an educated voice:

"*Merci, Madame* Blanc. That will be all!"

It was an order of dismissal, and Suzette was aware of it.

She gave Mimosa what was a frantic glance, then reluctantly walked back into the Villa.

Mimosa waited, deliberately making herself seem limp and not particularly interested in the new arrival.

"So you are back!" *Monsieur* Charlot said. "You must have had a very unpleasant experience with those criminals who abducted you."

"I . . . I do not . . . remember," Mimosa said faintly.

His lips curved in what she thought was a somewhat unpleasant smile.

"I doubt if that is entirely true, but it is a matter

of no particular consequence. I have come to talk to you again about what we were discussing the day before you vanished.''

Mimosa opened her eyes wide.

"Have I . . . met you . . . before?" she asked.

"You most certainly have!" *Monsieur* Charlot said. "Now, try to think sensibly, Miss Tison, about what I said to you when I came to see you after *Comte* André had left."

Mimosa was suddenly aware that he was speaking to her in English.

Suzette had, of course, talked French.

When *Monsieur* Charlot had sat down beside her, she was wondering why Suzette had warned her he was dangerous.

She had not at first realised that he was speaking in her own language.

He spoke English very well, but with an accent.

Now she wondered if he was speaking English for a purpose.

Was it in order to prevent Suzette from being able to overhear and understand what they were saying.

"I do not . . . remember talking . . . to you," Mimosa said slowly.

As this was true, there was a note of conviction in her voice which she felt *Monsieur* Charlot would not miss.

"Very well," he said, "then I will start again at the beginning. But I am quite certain, looking at you, that you are more intelligent than you appear to be. It is in fact very sensible of you not to remember what happened during your absence."

"Why . . . should you . . . say that?" Mimosa enquired.

"Because," he said, "if you do remember, you will be cross-examined continually by the Police. The French have no wish for these kidnappings and other acts of violence to continue to take place in Tunis."

He paused for a moment, and then went on:

"The more criminals they can catch and convict, the easier it is for them to keep the peace."

That, Mimosa thought, was common sense.

She was glad that she had been clever enough to appear to have lost her memory.

As *Monsieur* Charlot had said, she would not be troubled with continual questioning, and worse still, having to identify those who had taken Minerva away.

"Your abduction does not concern me," *Monsieur* Charlot continued, "but if you have forgotten what treatment you received from your kidnappers, you will not have forgotten André de Boussens."

Mimosa did not speak.

She was aware that he was looking at her penetratingly, expecting some reaction to the name, if it was only a flicker of the eye.

"As I told you before," *Monsieur* Charlot continued, "you hold his future in your hands. If you do not save him, his suffering will be far more severe than anything you have experienced."

"I . . . I do not . . . understand," Mimosa said again.

She was, in fact, finding it impossible to make

53

sense of what *Monsieur* Charlot was saying.

"Then let me put it a little more bluntly," *Monsieur* Charlot said. "You came to Paris with your Father and Mother because your Father had business with the President and a number of Bankers and other important people."

This did not surprise Mimosa.

She had known in the last years before her Mother died that, as Clint Tison was so rich, he had business interests in quite a number of European countries.

She could remember Minerva going with him to Spain and finding it fascinating.

She had spent a month in Italy also with her parents.

"Was it fun," Mimosa had asked.

Minerva, who had been sixteen at the time, had made a little grimace.

"It could have been," she said. "The Galleries and the Churches were beautiful, but Papa's friends . . ."

She threw out her hands in an expressive gesture.

". . . were all old and very serious. There were no exciting young Italian men to ask me to dance."

Mimosa had laughed, but she knew exacly what her Cousin was complaining about.

She had seen many of the men who had called to see Clint Tison at their house.

Once she had said to her Mother:

"I wonder, Mama, why it is that people who are concerned with business always look so serious, and most of them seem very old."

Her Mother had laughed.

"To them," she replied, "money is a very serious subject, and not to be taken lightly."

"But Uncle Clint is not always serious," Mimosa persisted.

"That is because he does not have to worry about money," her Mother answered. "It is worry that makes people old and gives them lines on their faces and white hair on their heads."

She kissed Mimosa and added:

"It will be a long time, my dearest, before you have to worry about money, so just enjoy yourself and forget it."

Monsieur Charlot was still talking.

"I had the privilege," he said, "of dining one night with your Father and Mother at the house which Mr. Tison had taken in the Rue St. Honoré. It was a large, very elite party to which only the most important people in Paris had been invited."

His voice became more impressive as he went on:

"The *Comte* André was there, and I saw when he looked at you that he was attracted, as a great many other men were. You are very beautiful, Miss Tison, and your beauty would turn the head of any man, especially one like *Comte* André, who is a connoisseur of beautiful women."

Mimosa made a little murmur, but did not interrupt.

"I was not surprised when my friends told me that the *Comte* made every excuse to see your Father—

and of course you. Then came disaster!''

He paused dramatically before he went on:

"It seems cruel that your Father and Mother should have perished in a railway accident in which only ten other people were killed and a large number escaped with minor injuries.''

Because she could not contain her curiosity, Mimosa asked in what she hoped was a bewildered tone:

"W-why had they . . . left Paris?''

"I should have thought you would have remembered that, if nothing else,'' *Monsieur* Charlot answered. "They went to Lyon just for the night because your Father had an important meeting there. But you stayed behind, having promised to go to the Opera in a party arranged by *Comte* André.''

Mimosa shook her head.

"I do not . . . remember,'' she whispered.

At the same time, she was fascinated by the story *Monsieur* Charlot was relating because he was telling her all the things she wanted to know.

She had thought it a mistake to ask too many questions of Suzette.

"You went to the Opera,'' *Monsieur* Charlot said, "and it was *Comte* André who comforted you later when you learnt what had happened to the two people you loved best in the world.''

"But . . . was I . . . alone in . . . Paris?'' Mimosa questioned.

"Of course not,'' *Monsieur* Charlot replied. "It had been arranged for a most respected and charming friend of the family, the *Comtesse* de Bizet, to stay with you in the house.''

"Then . . . why did . . . the *Comte* . . .'' Mimosa began.

"Comfort you?'' *Monsieur* Charlot finished. "Because you must be aware that he had fallen in love with you, and, as usual, when he saw a beautiful woman, he was determined to possess her.''

He gave a short laugh, and it was an unpleasant sound.

"You were trapped, my beautiful Miss Tison, as a great many other women have been trapped by *Comte* André's charm, and found it impossible to escape. He is known in Paris as the 'Man Who Has Broken a Thousand Hearts,' and yours was no exception.''

With difficulty, Mimosa bit back the questions which came to her lips.

Then, as if he read her thoughts, *Monsieur* Charlot continued:

"I do not know how soon you realised that he was a married man. It is something he keeps from his victim until she is helplessly enamoured and cannot escape from the magic which makes her so pliable in his hands.''

"Suzette . . . told me he was . . . married,'' Mimosa murmured.

"Suzette Blanc,'' *Monsieur* Charlot said scornfully, "is one of the idiot women who loved him when she was young and has continued to love him in a ridiculous manner which has ruined her life.''

"How has it ruined her?'' Mimosa enquired.

"Because, Miss Tison, while she is older than *Comte* André, she is undoubtedly a pretty woman, and she left her family, who were respectable *Bourgeois,* to crawl at his feet!''

He seemed almost to spit out the words, and as Mimosa stared at him, he said:

"He used her, of course he used her. Is there any woman whom André de Boussens has not used in one way or another? She procured for him the pretty girls he wanted when he was no longer interested in her as a woman.''

He stopped talking a moment, then went on:

"Her parents would have nothing to do with her. They were so shocked at her behaviour and her hopeless infatuation for a man who quite obviously was using her for his own purposes and for no other reason.''

Mimosa drew in her breath.

How could Minerva, her sweet, gentle Cousin, love a man like that?

"Women, it was just women *Comte* André required,'' *Monsieur* Charlot was saying, "but his interest in them never lasted.''

There was a sneer on his lips as he continued:

"In your case, of course, it was not only your beauty that held him, but your money. Women are expensive, especially when a man has no money of his own, and has to rely on his wife for everything he wants.''

Mimosa thought what he was saying was so horrible that she did not want to listen.

Yet, if she told *Monsieur* Charlot to be quiet and go away, it would be difficult to keep up her pretence of not being able to remember anything that had happened in the past.

She could only be still and feel hypnotised by the way he spoke, and what he was saying.

"It was your money, Miss Tison," *Monsieur* Charlot went on, "that made André de Boussens bring you here to Tunis. Her persuaded his wife, who is a relative of the President's, that he should come to Tunisia to help in the administration of this country."

He stopped for a moment, looking at Mimosa intently before he went on:

"She, of course, had no idea that he intended to take you with him from Paris, and persuade you to buy this delightful Villa in which to accommodate him, as well as yourself."

Monsieur Charlot looked round as he spoke.

There was an expression in his eyes which made Mimosa feel as if a cold hand clutched at her heart.

It was obvious that *Monsieur* Charlot hated the *Comte*.

She was also certain that he was determined to hurt her in some way.

"*Comte* André," *Monsieur* Charlot was saying, "manipulated his wife just as cleverly as he manipulated you and all the other women who groveled at his feet. She thought it would be good for him to be away from Paris for a while. She may, who knows, have thought you were a danger. Which actually you were, although she had survived a thousand such dangers already.''

''I . . . I do not . . . understand,'' Mimosa managed to say when he seemed to pause deliberately.

''I think you do, Miss Tison,'' *Monsieur* Charlot said. ''*Comte* André must have told you that without his wife's support and her influential relatives he would undoubtedly be an outcast of French Society.''

He laughed again before he said:

''But André outwitted them, as he always does. He came to Tunis but brought you with him to make him comfortable and to purchase for him everything he fancied.''

He paused and then continued:

''It took some time before people in Paris were aware that his behaviour here was not what they had expected, or what the President himself had intended. The French intention is to raise morale in Tunis, not to flout the conventions, as the *Comte* was doing in living openly with you.''

He saw the expression on Mimosa's face and said:

''Oh, I know he brought Suzette with him, but that was only a blind which deceived no-one. The French are well aware of her reputation.''

''I do not . . . think . . .'' Mimosa managed to say, ''that I . . . want to hear . . . any more.''

''You asked for the whole story, and now you have to listen to it,'' *Monsieur* Charlot said. ''In case he did not tell you the truth, which is something very alien to his nature, he was recalled because the report had at length reached Paris that he was living in your house and spending money extravagantly in a country where they were endeavouring to set an example of decency.''

Mimosa was silent as he went on:

''The President had promised to clean up the scandals that had been rife before we came in and restored order. It was the President who insisted that *Comte* André return home. At the same time, the President was considerate enough not to let his Cousin, the *Comtesse* de Boussens, know the reason for her husband's return.''

Because she could not help herself, Mimosa murmured:

''Suzette . . . told me that . . . it was *Madame la Comtesse* who . . . demanded that . . . the *Comte* should . . . go back.''

''Suzette Blanc is talking nonsense,'' *Monsieur* Charlot said. ''I can assure you, as I have just come from Paris, that the *Comte* is happily reunited with his wife, who had no idea that his affair with you, Miss Tison, was causing so much scandal in Tunis that the President was informed of it.''

There was nothing Mimosa could say, and she remained silent.

Then *Monsieur* Charlot said in a different tone:

''That is where you come in.''

She looked at him in a perplexed manner, and he explained:

''If you love *Comte* André, and I am sure, like every other woman, you love him deeply and with your whole heart, then you will want his wife to believe his lies and that he should not be exposed as the devil he really is.''

Again he was almost spitting out the words.

It was clear from the expression in his eyes how much he hated the *Comte*.

"What . . . are you . . . saying? What . . . do you . . . want me to do?" Mimosa managed to ask.

"I should have thought that was obvious," *Monsieur* Charlot answered. "I want money, Miss Tison, money to keep my lips sealed where your lover is concerned. Money to stop me from showing *Madame la Comtesse* your letters which I have obtained from their house in Paris.''

He waved his hand as he held them and finished:

"Letters to ensure that the Prodigal has returned home and for the moment nothing will be said about what he had been doing during his absence.''

There was no doubt now that *Monsieur* Charlot was looking like the evil man he really was.

Mimosa knew that, as Suzette had warned her, he was dangerous.

It was best, she thought, not to speak.

She merely shut her eyes as if she were too tired or too bemused to understand what he was saying.

She knew, however, that he was looking at her, staring at her, and she felt him willing her to obey him.

It was almost as if he were mesmerising her into doing so.

It was with an effort that she forced herself to keep quiet.

She tried to keep her hands still in her lap, and her head back on the cushion behind her.

"What I want," *Monsieur* Charlot said slowly, "is fifty thousand *francs* to save your lover. If you do not let me have it, I will go straight from here to *Madame la Comtesse*. She will have the letters that will tell her the truth of what has happened."

He waited and, as Mimosa did not speak, he continued:

"My informants, who are very shrewd, tell me that the last time an episode like this came to light, the *Comte* swore on the Bible that he would never behave in such a manner again, or do anything to disgrace the name of de Boussens."

He paused for breath before he went on:

"If *Madame* de Boussens learns that he had broken his vow and brought shame on her and his children, she will leave him. Then there will be nothing for him to do but kill himself, or else starve in the gutter!"

Monsieur Charlot was speaking to her in a low voice.

Yet Mimosa felt as if he were shouting the words aloud and they were echoing round the garden.

She could understand only too well what he was saying.

Her Father had told her how proud the French were of their family name.

How those belonging to the *ancien régime* would

63

never allow a breath of scandal to poison their reputation.

She thought it appalling that her Cousin, whom she loved so deeply, should have lived with any man in sin.

That it should be with a man like the *Comte,* who was obviously a *Roué* and a seducer of women, made her want to cry.

She loved Minerva, but she had been cosseted and indulged by her Father and Mother.

She had never encountered the harsh world outside her sheltered and luxurious home.

She would not understand a man like *Comte* André.

She would have had no idea that he was a "Wolf in Sheep's Clothing," a destroyer of the women who loved him.

As if he were impatient at her silence, *Monsieur* Charlot asked:

"Well, what is your answer. Do I get the money, or do I go to the *Comtesse*?"

"I . . . think," Mimosa answered, "you are . . . blackmailing me."

Monsieur Charlot laughed the same unpleasant laugh which was a sound with no humour in it.

"I prefer to think," he said, "that I am doing the man you love a kindness. If these letters I now possess had fallen into the hands of anybody else, they might already have appeared in the Press. They are very loving and very passionate."

He made the last words sound almost insults.

"I am sure you will remember, if you think about

it long enough. And I cannot believe that your Father, who was so respected both in England and America, as well as in France, would have been pleased if he knew what enormous amounts of his money had been spent by one of the most raffish men Paris has ever known.''

That, at least, Mimosa thought, was true.

She was aware that Clint Tison had adored his daughter, just as he had adored his wife.

It would be impossible for him to believe that either of them could do anything wrong, certainly nothing so degrading as living with a man as his wife when he was already married, a man who apparently collected women as other men collected stamps.

''What . . . shall . . . I do? What . . . can I . . . answer?'' Mimosa asked herself frantically.

Then she realised that because she had kept her eyes closed and had not moved, *Monsieur* Charlot was somewhat disconcerted.

She knew he was looking at her closely, wondering if what he had said had penetrated her brain.

Had she really understood the enormous sum of money he had demanded of her?

He waited.

It was with a great effort that Mimosa did not look at him.

Finally he said:

''I will give you three days in which to think it over. I have other business while I am here, and that will give you time to consider.''

Mimosa still made no reply.

"It will also give you time to obtain the money in cash from the Bank. I am not so stupid as to want there to be any evidence against me, or that it should be known by anyone that I am accepting money from you."

His voice rose a little as he said:

"You do understand, Miss Tison, what I am saying? I want that money, and I want you to hand it to me without anyone, least of all Suzette Blanc, being aware that I have received it. Do you hear? Answer me!"

It was a command, and Mimosa now could not help opening her eyes.

His face was very near to hers, and she thought she could see the evil in his eyes.

She knew he was willing her.

He was almost compelling her to accept what he had said.

Because she was frightened, her voice seemed to tremble as she answered:

"I . . . I am . . . listening . . . I will . . . think of . . . what you have . . . said."

"Very well—think!" *Monsieur* Charlot told her. "And remember, if I do not get the answer I require and receive the money, then *Comte* André will suffer, and compared to what you have suffered, he will suffer all the agonies of hell."

As he finished speaking, he rose from his chair and walked away.

He crossed the patio and entered the house.

Mimosa could hear Suzette Blanc talking to him, her voice sounding high and excited.

She clasped her hands together and looked out over the garden.

It was still there, beautiful and sun-kissed.

The bees were humming over the flowers and the birds were fluttering in the trees.

It was very beautiful, but there was a serpent in the Garden of Eden, and she did not know how to cope with it.

chapter four

THE Duke of Alrock arrived in Paris and went straight to the house in the Champs-Élysées where he always stayed with his friend the *Vicomte* de Flerry.

After they had enjoyed a glass of champagne and discussed the political situation in both their countries, the *Vicomte* said:

"Tonight I am taking you to a party."

The Duke groaned.

"I would much rather have had dinner with you," he said, "at Maxim's for preference."

"We can go there another night, but I think you will find this particular party something very special."

The Duke raised his eye-brows a little cynically.

He knew what a "special" party in Paris meant,

and he told himself he was not at the moment at all interested.

"It is being given," his friend was saying, "by one of the richest Bankers in Paris, who is determined to out-spend and out-shine any other party to which his guests have been invited.

"I doubt that," the Duke replied laconically. "You know as well as I do, Henri, that just as all roads lead to Rome, all parties in Paris lead to bed!"

The *Vicomte* laughed. Then he said:

"Well, I insist on your coming with me, but if you decide to go home early, that is your business."

There was nothing the Duke could do but agree to participate.

He thought, however, it would be the sort of orgy he had attended dozens of times in his younger days.

He had always found Paris fascinating, but especially so when he had come there first, soon after coming down from Oxford.

He had then been bewildered, entranced, and fascinated by the exotic Courtesans.

Glittering with diamonds, they competed with each other to display themselves in the *Bois* more sensationally than any other Professional had ever done before.

But they also, he thought, helped a man to forget any troubles and any difficulties he had brought with him to Paris.

That did not really apply to him at the moment.

At the same time, he had left England knowing it was a wise thing to do if he wished to finish an *affaire-de-coeur* which had burnt itself out.

He had found Lady Sybil Brooke amusing and witty, and insatiable where love-making was concerned.

Yet, as he grew to know her better, he had decided she was trying to play too big a part in his life.

The simplest way to avoid directly telling her so, he thought, was to go abroad.

The Duke had long ago decided that he would not marry until he was very much older.

He had seen a number of his friends of the same social standing as himself being marched up the aisle by ambitious Mamas.

It was usually before they had had time to enjoy themselves as bachelors.

Because he was intelligent, he reasoned out carefully that he would first enjoy the freedom every young unmarried man should have.

Then he would settle down and have a family.

He would have been very foolish, which he was not, if he had been unaware that he was one of the most important matrimonial catches in the whole of the Social World.

His Father had always been treated like a King on his own Estate and in his own country.

His position at Court was traditional in his family.

It had been filled by the last three Dukes of Alrock and ten Earls in the family before them.

They had served their country in many different ways.

As Statesmen they were outstanding, while the

10th Earl had been indispensable to Marlborough in his Campaigns.

The Duke was very conscious of his social position.

At the same time, he was genuinely interested in politics and international affairs, in fact more so than even his Father had been.

As a Peer, it was of course impossible for him to become a Member of the House of Commons.

He had therefore turned his attention to foreign affairs.

He had made himself an expert in the politics of the countries of the western world and in any ambitions they might have on the international scene.

Because he had no wish to appear over-curious, he had taken up Archaeology as a cover and had in fact become very knowledgeable on the Roman Empire.

This interest took him into a large number of countries without appearing to pry into their internal politics.

He, however, learned a great deal about them while ostensibly examining what was left of Roman Cities, Temples, Aqueducts, and Roads.

He had, in fact, become so involved in this study that he was compiling a book on it.

He hoped to have it published the following year.

He was now dressing with the help of his Valet, who travelled everywhere with his Master.

As he did so, he was thinking that the party tonight would be a complete waste of his time.

He would rather have gone to bed early and set

off again on his travels the next morning.

"What have you unpacked, Jenkins?" he asked his Valet.

"Only wot Your Grace requires for this evening," Jenkins replied.

"That was sensible, as I think perhaps we might leave tomorrow."

The Duke spoke in a casual way, and his Valet looked at him sharply.

He knew only too well that his Master was not particularly pleased at having to go out that night.

At the same time, he thought perhaps it would be good for him to have a change of scene after what had happened in London.

Whoever it was who said that nothing could be kept a secret from the servants had been extremely shrewd.

Jenkins had known without being told that the Duke was running away from Lady Sybil.

He was sure it was for the simple reason that his Master could not stop her from trying by every means in her power to lure him into matrimony.

Lady Sybil had been a widow for three years.

She was determined again to marry someone who could give her the money she wanted and the life she enjoyed.

She also desired an unassailable position in the Social World.

Her Father had not been a very important Peer.

With little money, it was therefore imperative that Lady Sybil should find herself an important husband.

She had married a man who was very much older than herself, but was rich enough to please her Father.

Colonel Brooke, however, had no intention of spending his time in London.

He found the Balls, the parties, the Receptions, and the people who attended them boring.

He took his wife to the country, and Lady Sybil had become so frustrated that she sulked for weeks.

The only diversions were the horses and hunting in the Winter, and the shooting.

Her husband's friends were all the same age as himself, and their conversation seldom deviated from sport.

Lady Sybil thought she would go mad with the boredom of it all.

When her husband died unexpectedly of a heart-attack, she had difficulty in not dancing on his grave.

His relations had forced her to mourn him respectfully in public, while they whispered about her heartlessness in private.

When at last she was free to throw off her black crepe, she sped to London like a wild duck flighting in from the sea.

She opened her husband's London house, which he had kept closed all the time they were married.

She entertained wildly, luxuriously, and very extravagantly.

Her guests largely comprised those who could enjoy a good dinner without having to pay for it and who found a pretty woman irresistible.

It was as soon as Lady Sybil had seen the Duke

for the first time that she knew what she wanted and what she intended to have.

She stalked him more persistently than any Scottish stalker ever followed a stag.

When he finally succumbed, she thought she had achieved her objective and won what had been an arduous battle.

The Duke was everything she desired as a lover.

Yet she could not persuade him to say the words she longed to hear, the words which would make her his wife.

Nor, she was aware, did he ever actually say "I love you!"

It took her some time to understand, for she was not very perceptive, that what he enjoyed with her was not love as the word meant to him.

It took a long time, in fact many sleepless nights, before she faced the unpleasant truth.

While the Duke enjoyed her as a woman, she made no impact on his brain, nor on what she thought of as his heart.

He was courteous, good-mannered, and grateful in his own way for the pleasure she gave him.

He sent her flowers and presents of no particular value, but which were in good taste, appropriate presents for a woman who thought of herself as a Lady.

She knew when he left her as dawn was breaking that she was never quite certain if she would see him again.

She wondered if he would disappear without even realising how much she would miss him.

Sometimes she felt like screaming at him because in spite of all her efforts, he remained out of reach.

She tried being slightly elusive, but that did not work.

She then determined to make herself indispensable to him.

She had to make him feel that life would be impossible without her.

That was where she made her fatal mistake.

The Duke woke up to the fact that Lady Sybil was becoming too familiar, too demanding, and too possessive.

That was the one word that frightened him.

He had no wish to be possessed by anybody, least of all by somebody whose whole mind was fixed on matrimony.

Impulsively, making a quick decision, which was characteristic of him, he told his Valet to pack.

They left London the following day.

He knew his Secretary could cope with everything, including the engagements for which he had to apologise, and, of course, Lady Sybil.

The Duke ordered a basket of flowers to be sent to her as well as a polite note.

In it he said how sorry he was not to be able to dine with her that evening as he had promised.

He explained:

> *"I have to go to Paris, then on for a visit to Tunisia, where I wish to see some Roman ruins and include an account of them in my book.*

"I know you will understand, and I thank you again for all the delightful times we have spent together . . ."

When Lady Sybil found the note lying on her breakfast-tray, she felt apprehensive.

It was unlike the Duke to write to her when he had seen her only the previous evening.

He had escorted her home early, saying that he was tired, which also was unlike him.

In fact, she was sure because he was so athletic and strong, that he was never tired.

She had said to him in a tone of concern:

"You do not think you have a cold?"

"I hope not," the Duke had replied, "but I want an early night."

He had taken her back to her house.

To her annoyance, he had kissed her goodnight without much warmth in the carriage.

He had then said goodbye on the doorstep.

She could hardly beg to come in in front of the Night-Footman.

She therefore simply said:

"I am sure you would like a night-cap, and there is some champagne in the Drawing-Room."

She looked up at him, as she spoke, with an expression in her eyes which he could not misunderstand.

"Thank you," he replied, "but not tonight."

Before she could think of anything more to say, he had stepped back into his carriage.

As he drove off, she wanted to run after him.

She felt in some inexplicable way that he was driving out of her life.

As she now read the note she knew that was exactly what he had done.

The Duke had actually thought about Lady Sybil several times as he was crossing the Channel.

His Secretary had, as usual, arranged everything with a speed and expertise that the Duke had come to expect of him.

His Grace had the best cabin on the ship, and a coupe reserved for him on the train to Paris.

He read the newspapers and thought of what he would see in Tunis.

He felt with the satisfaction of a boy going home for the holidays that he was free, free of Lady Sybil's demands of her incessant notes which arrived nearly every day on her scented writing-paper.

He was free of her constant demands on his manhood which he had begun to find excessive.

Just for the moment he felt he had had enough of women, which was the reason he was not at all pleased by the *Vicomte*'s plans for the evening.

He told himself he must be getting old.

Five years ago he would have been excited by the idea of meeting the *crème de la crème* of the Parisian Courtesans.

They were the most famous in the whole of Europe.

"What is wrong with me? What do I want?" he asked himself as many men had asked before him.

He did not know the answer.

Quite suddenly it struck him that perhaps he had

become an idealist through his new interest in Roman culture springing from his study of Roman ruins.

Was he looking for Aphrodite, as the Greeks called the Goddess of Love?

Or perhaps it was the Venus of the Romans, with her exquisite body and a face that was more saintly than sensual.

"The Gods of Olympus!"

He laughed aloud at the idea.

He had, however, never met a woman who could rival those creatures of ancient mythology who had appeared on the "shining cliffs" at Delphi or in the Temples he had inspected in a number of different countries.

Jenkins helped him into his well-fitting evening-coat.

It had been made by the best and most expensive tailor in Savile Row.

The Duke took a perfunctory look at himself in the mirror.

He had no idea how handsome he was, or that, more important, he had a personality which vibrated out from him to everyone with whom he came in contact.

Jenkins handed him a considerable sum of money which he put into the inside pocket of his coat.

There were also some gold *louis* to go into his trouser-pocket.

Automatically, although the Duke knew it was unnecessary, he said:

"I will not be late, Jenkins, but do not wait up."

"You're certain Your Grace won't want me?"

"Quite certain!" the Duke said firmly.

He walked towards the bedroom door, and the Valet opened it for him.

As his Master disappeared down the corridor, Jenkins looked at his own reflection in the mirror and said aloud:

"What's the bettin' 'Is Nibs' don't return before dawn's breakin'!"

Then he laughed out loud.

An hour later, the Duke was sitting at the dinner-table in a large and luxurious house in the Rue St. Honoré.

He was aware that his friend the *Vicomte* had not exaggerated in saying that this was to be a superlative party.

There was no doubt that the women were some of the most beautiful he had seen anywhere, and that included Paris itself.

The whole room was decorated with orchids.

When they sat down at the table, in front of every woman's plate were two perfect orchids, just touched with pink, bound together by a thousand-franc note.

The cuisine was perfection.

The meal started with caviar which had been specially brought from Russia for the occasion.

The courses that succeeded it were the most superlative of French artistry.

The wines, as only the men knew, were of vintages so rare and so fine that they should have been drunk reverently by the spoonful rather than in glasses.

The Duke was aware that the male guests consisted of the most important men in Paris.

Their host, the Banker, had an international reputation.

He was so rich that it was doubtful if the evening's entertainment would even cause him to look twice at the bill.

He had excelled himself this evening.

While they were eating, a Violinist who was considered the finest in Europe played softly in the background.

The party consisted of just thirty people.

It was difficult to find words adequate to describe the attractions of the Courtesan on his left.

She was dark-haired with a magnolia skin and huge eyes that seemed to glitter like diamonds.

She was also witty, and he found himself laughing at everything she said.

She managed by some charm of her own to make the very air sparkle with a *joie de vivre* which was peculiarly French.

On his right sat a woman who was half-Swedish.

Her hair was so pale that if her eyes had been pink, she would have been an albino.

Instead, they were strikingly green and turned up at the corners.

Her voice was very soft.

She had a way of making everything she said seem intimate, as if she were talking for his ears alone.

Without being conscious of it, the Duke found himself responding to her with pleasure.

She was, however, being monopolised by the man on her other side.

He therefore turned back to the woman on his left.

Once again she was making him laugh.

When he asked her name she said:

"I am known as *La Belle*."

"It suits you," he replied.

They talked and laughed as they moved into another room to dance to an orchestra specially engaged from Vienna.

It had been transformed into a bower of white roses.

He realised it was a flattering background for the beautiful women who had been invited.

Still more surprises awaited them.

There was an actor from the Theatre who sang *risqué,* but at the same time cleverly amusing, songs.

An Acrobat, whose act was short but brilliant, vanished with everybody shouting for more.

There was a cotillion in which extremely rich and expensive presents were provided to be given by the men to the women with whom they danced.

Then, almost before anybody had had time to breathe, there were fireworks in the garden.

They turned the sky into a kaleidoscope of colour such as the Duke had never seen before.

As soon as the fireworks began, *La Belle* took him by the hand and led him into the garden.

Little grottoes had been arranged round a fountain that stood in the centre of the lawn.

The grottoes were small and the Duke realised there were exactly fifteen of them.

They were all fashioned of exquisite flowers.

They hung in each from a curved ceiling over a couch draped with velvet onto which rose-petals fell slowly, one by one.

Tiny lights were hidden behind the flowers, and there was an exotic fragrance in the air.

As the fireworks ended, a Gypsy Band, which the Duke was sure had come from Hungary, started playing in the garden.

It was the exotic, compelling, entrancing music of passion, which only the Gypsies knew.

Yet it was irresistible to all who heard it.

Almost like a dream *La Belle* moved into the Duke's arms, and they sank together onto the softness of a rose-petal-covered couch.

As the Duke went home in the early hours of the morning, he thought with a twist of his lips that Henri had been right when he had said it would be a "party to end all parties," that it would be a mistake for him to be in Paris and deny himself the pleasure of enjoying it.

Nothing in fact, could exceed what he had enjoyed that night.

But the sooner he was on his way the better.

He especially remembered a conversation he had had with one of the other guests before going in to dinner.

The man had introduced himself, saying:

"We have met before, *Monsieur le Duc,* but I

doubt if you remember me.''

The Duke, who had an extremely good memory, only hesitated for a moment before he said:

"Of course I remember you, *Comte* André, and it is nice to see you again."

"I am flattered that you have not forgotten," the *Comte* said.

They had met at a dinner given by the President which in fact the Duke had found rather dull.

He remembered also that the *Comte* was married to the President's cousin, and he asked genially:

"How is *Madame la Comtesse*? In good health I hope?"

"Excellent, thank you," *Comte* André replied, "and may I ask the obvious question as to why you are in Paris?"

The Duke smiled.

"I am only passing through and I am actually leaving for Tunis tomorrow."

"Tunis!" *Comte* André exclaimed. "I was there a short time ago."

He paused, then he said:

"Can it be that you are interested in Thuburbo Maius? I thought you would have seen it before now."

"I have hardly had the opportunity," the Duke replied, "considering that your countrymen have only recently got the Tunisians under control, and I am told that visitors are now welcome."

"I am sure they will welcome you," *Comte* André said.

He paused for a moment before he said:

"I think, unless you have other arrangements, you may find the Hotels somewhat uncomfortable."

The Duke shrugged his shoulders.

"I suppose that is what I must expect, but I am hoping that the food will be French."

Comte André was writing something on a piece of paper.

"Let me suggest," he said, "you visit the Villa *l'Astre Bleu,* which was very comfortable and the food was excellent."

He saw that the Duke looked puzzled, and he explained:

"It is where I stayed myself, and it belongs to a friend of mine. You may have met her—the great Heiress, Minerva Tison."

The Duke wrinkled his forehead.

"Tison? Tison? Surely he died in an accident a short time ago?"

"Sadly that is so," the *Comte* answered. "His daughter is very lovely and very charming but now all on her own. It would really be a kindness if you called on her, and I am sure she would welcome any friend of mine."

He smiled before he added:

". . . and give her my love!"

The way he spoke told the Duke a great deal without putting it into words.

He put the note into his pocket and said:

"Thank you, it is very kind of you. I will certainly convey your message to Miss Tison, even if I do not impose on her as a guest."

"It is something I strongly advise you to do," the

Comte said reflectively. ''The Hotels, such as they are, are not yet 'Frenchified,' to coin a word. The food is dubious, and the service from Tunisians almost non-existent.''

''Now you are frightening me!'' the Duke complained.

''I am offering you the alternative of the Villa *l'Astre Bleu*,'' the *Comte* said.

The Duke's attention was then claimed by his host and he did not get a chance to speak to the *Comte* again.

Now, while he was sailing towards Tunis, he was thinking about the conversation.

He decided he would be extremely stupid if he did not at least investigate the *Comte*'s suggestion.

He was not particularly impressed by the *Comte* himself.

At the same time, he was aware that having been invited as a guest at that particular party he would appreciate comfort.

He was doubtless right when he said that the Hotels in Tunis were not yet ''Frenchified.''

But they soon would be.

The French, when they took over a country, did it with an admirable expertise.

The Duke knew that in a very short time the food would be superb and the service in the Hotels excellent.

The good manners of the French were one of their strongest exports.

''I shall certainly try to win my way into the Villa,'' he decided.

The sea was calm, the sun was shining, and the white houses of Tunis looked very attractive as the ship came into Port.

The Duke knew that the famous City of Carthage had been utterly destroyed by the Romans.

He had been told there was nothing left of it to see except traces of the harbour.

But the Roman provincial town of Thuburbo Maius, which had only just started to be excavated, would certainly have a place in his book.

As the ship docked soon after he had had breakfast, he told himself he would certainly try first the Villa *l'Astre Bleu*.

Should that fail, he would go into the Town and try to find something that was at least habitable.

There was the usual crowd of natives offering to act as guides to the passengers as they stepped down the gangplank.

They offered for sale coins which they claimed had come from ancient Carthage.

There were pieces of stone which no-one in their right mind could possibly wish to possess.

The Duke brushed them aside.

Jenkins, having found a Porter to carry the baggage, hurriedly secured a Hackney-Carriage.

It was certainly not a vehicle which would have passed muster in Paris.

The carriage itself looked as if it were a hundred years old.

The horse was obviously tired and had no wish to hurry from the harbour.

Jenkins climbed up on the box, and by some miraculous means of his own alerted the driver to move a little more quickly.

He, however, started to grumble when they reached Sidi Bou Said and began the long haul up the winding road.

The Duke thought that because it was steep he would doubtless be expected to pay more than if his destination had been nearer sea-level.

He was intent on noticing the fragrance of syringa, the bushes and the trees brilliant with blossom.

Then there was the shining whiteness of the few Villas at the foot of the hill.

It seemed a strange place for a young American woman like Miss Tison to live, especially now that she was alone since the death of her Father and Mother in the train accident.

He had questioned the *Vicomte* before he left Paris.

"It was a tragedy!" the *Vicomte* said. "Tison was brilliant! He had a creative brain and everyone wanted not only his money, but also his advice. He was a Visionary, and so shrewd that everything he touched turned to gold."

"I wish I had met him," the Duke said.

"He was a handsome man and his wife was lovely, in fact one of the most beautiful women I have ever seen."

"She was American?" the Duke asked.

"I suppose so," the *Vicomte* answered. "She was very retiring and seldom appeared in public."

Now, as the conversation came back to him, he realised that the wretched horse was sweating as the hill became steeper and steeper.

Then suddenly they came to a halt.

They were outside some imposing gates.

Through them the Duke could see the Villa surrounded by a blaze of colour.

Jenkins got down from the box to open the gate for him.

"Keep the carriage," the Duke said, "and wait for me here. I have first to find out whether we will be welcome, or if we have to return to the City."

"I'm keepin' me fingers crossed, Your Grace," Jenkins replied.

chapter five

MIMOSA awoke early, and the *femme de chambre* who came to call her said:

"*Madame* Blanc is not well this morning. She is staying in bed with a migraine."

"Oh, I am sorry," Mimosa exclaimed.

Actually she was rather glad.

She found Suzette's incessant chatter exhausting.

When she had breakfasted she felt for the first time that she was free and on her own.

She therefore went to the cupboard, where she had placed the manuscript of her Father's book which had arrived at the Villa the day after she had.

She had fortunately been alone when the man-servant brought it to her.

As she had no wish to make long explanations to

Suzette, she had put it hastily away in a cupboard in the Sitting-Room.

Now she took the parcel out and opened it.

The moment she saw her Father's hand-writing, she felt the tears come into her eyes.

It was with difficulty that she read what he had written about Thuburbo Maius.

It was certainly very interesting, and he had already done a lot of work on it before he died from the snake-bite.

She spread out the pages on a table and started to read how Thuburbo Maius had developed first as a Numidion City and had sided with Carthage in the final Punic War.

Her Father had learnt all that was known about it before they had visited the actual site.

He was certain that when the ruins were finally unearthed, there would be a new chapter in the Archaeologists' knowledge of the Romans.

She was sorting out his notes which she had not yet written up for him in her clear hand-writing, when the door opened.

"Il y a un Monsieur pour vous voir, M'mselle," a servant said.

Mimosa looked up in surprise as a man she had never seen before came into the room.

She was aware that he was very smartly dressed.

He was young, good-looking, and she was sure even before he spoke that he was an Englishman.

The Duke was staring at her in astonishment.

He had been told by *Comte* André that her Mother was beautiful.

But the girl facing him was indisputably one of the loveliest women he had ever seen.

The sun was turning her hair to gold, and as she looked at him he saw that her eyes were the pale blue of a Summer sky.

He also noted that she was frightened.

He thought it strange that she should be afraid of him, and he said quickly:

"Good morning, Miss Tison. May I apologise for intruding and introduce myself? I am the Duke of Alrock, and I have come to Tunis to inspect the Roman ruins, recently uncovered, of Thuburbo Maius."

As he was speaking, Mimosa had risen to her feet and the Duke went on:

"I have come from Paris on my way here, and I bring messages to you from *Comte* André de Boussens."

He expected from what the *Comte* had told him that this statement would be received enthusiastically.

Again, to his surprise, Mimosa's eyes flickered and he saw the colour rising in her cheeks.

Her skin was exquisitely white and he thought the blush was like the first sign of the sun at dawn and quite as beautiful.

With what he was aware was an effort, she said politely:

"Will you not . . . sit down, and perhaps . . . you would . . . like some . . . refreshment?"

"I have just had a very nasty breakfast on the ship which brought me here," the Duke replied, "and if it is no trouble, I would greatly appreciate some coffee.''

"Of course," Mimosa said.

She rang the bell, and as the man-servant appeared almost immediately, she guessed he must have been waiting for her summons in the hall.

"*Nous avons du café, s'il vous plaît*," she ordered.

She went nearer to the Duke and sat down on a chair facing him.

"So you have come to see the ruins at Thuburbo Maius," she said. "I think you will find them fascinating."

"You have seen them?" he asked in surprise.

Without thinking Mimosa replied:

"Oh, yes."

Then she remembered that it was very unlikely that her Cousin would have gone there.

She looked apprehensively at her Father's book which lay on the table.

The Duke followed the direction of her eyes.

He could not help seeing the words THUBURBO MAIUS written in large capital letters on the top sheet of a pile of paper.

He rose to his feet, saying:

"You actually have some notes on the City! Who has written them?"

There was a pause before Mimosa managed to reply:

"M-my . . . Uncle . . . Sir Richard Shenson."

She spoke unsteadily, and the Duke stared at her.

"Richard Shenson is your Uncle?" he enquired.

"I had no idea of it. I knew your Father was American, and I had the idea that your Mother was American too."

"Oh, no," Mimosa said. "She was English."

She did not explain any further, but the Duke was intent on looking at her Father's manuscript.

"You may think I am presuming," he said after a moment, "but I would be exceedingly grateful if you, or, rather, your Uncle, would allow me to read what he has written."

"My . . . my Uncle is . . . dead," Mimosa said.

"Dead?" the Duke exclaimed. "I am sorry to hear that. But he wrote all this before he died?"

"Yes," Mimosa agreed.

She was thinking to herself that she had to be very careful not to say too much, or to make him in the least suspicious as to who she really was.

Then she told herself that she was being ridiculous.

He knew her as "Miss Tison," and why should he suspect she was anyone else?

Anyway, he was only a stranger.

The Duke was staring down at the papers spread out on the table.

Then he said:

"When I was in Paris, Miss Tison, I met the *Comte* André de Boussens whom I had met once before. He told me you were a friend of his and that he had stayed with you while he was here in Tunis."

He paused a moment, but when she remained silent, he continued:

"I was wondering, although it may seem presumptuous, if you would accept me as your lodger, as I understand he was."

It was the last thing Mimosa had expected him to say, and for a moment she could only stare at him.

Then before she could speak he smiled.

"I have taken you by surprise," he said, "and I am sure you think it is extraordinary of me to barge my way in here without a proper introduction."

She did not answer, and he went on:

"I have never been in Tunis before, and I have the suspicion that the Hotels will be very uncomfortable and the food appalling."

As if she could not help it, Mimosa laughed.

"I am . . . sure that is . . . true."

"Then you will understand why I am pleading with you to be kind to an alien in a foreign country."

"I . . . I suppose," Mimosa said falteringly, "you could . . . stay here."

Even as she spoke she thought that it would somehow be a relief to have an English person with her.

He would be someone to talk to as a change from Suzette's endless chatter, and she could speak to him in her own language.

As if the Duke understood her hesitation, he said:

"I promise I will be no trouble, and, of course, as soon as I can arrange it, I want to go to Thuburbo Maius which I understand is some distance from Tunis."

"You will need to hire camel drivers to take

you," Mimosa said, "with a tent for you to sleep in."

"I can organise that," the Duke said, "but it would be of inestimable help, Miss Tison, if you could recommend whom I should engage. I believe many of the camel-drivers are thieves, and when one sets off into the uninhabited part of the country, there is always the chance that one will never return."

Mimosa did not answer.

She was thinking that her Father would never return, although it was through no fault of the camel-drivers.

The Duke was silent for a moment before he said:

"My luggage and my Valet are waiting outside your gates. I feel the driver of the dilapidated Hackney-Carriage which brought me here from the dock will be impatient to be paid."

The way he spoke sounded so amusing that Mimosa gave a little chuckle before she said:

"Then of course you must pay him, and the servants will bring in your luggage."

"Then I may stay?" the Duke asked.

"At least until you set off for Thuburbo Maius," Mimosa agreed.

"Before I do that," the Duke answered, "I must of course read your Uncle's book."

He smiled at her and walked to the door just as the man-servant appeared with the coffee.

"You had better let my servant Jacques pay the driver for you," Mimosa suggested, "and he will

97

tell your Valet that you are staying here. Then you can drink your coffee while it is still hot."

"I think that is a very sensible idea," the Duke said.

He took some money out of his pocket and gave it to Jacques.

He also told him in French to arrange with his Valet to bring in the luggage.

Mimosa was pouring out the coffee, and when the Duke took his cup from her, he sat down in a chair.

It was near the open window, and he looked at the garden, appreciating the beauty of the flowers.

"This is the most charming Villa I have ever seen!" he said. "And your garden is perfection!"

Mimosa said nothing.

She felt guilty at accepting a compliment about the Villa which she did not own and a garden which owed nothing to her effort and care.

She began wondering nervously if she had been wise in accepting the Duke as a guest.

At the same time, he gave her a sense of security she had not felt since she first arrived.

He was English, and perhaps in some way she could not yet fathom, he would help her to decide the best way she could return to England.

"I understand that *Comte* André was helping the French in their usual efficient way to administer the City," the Duke said conversationally.

To his surprise, Mimosa blushed and said hastily:

"We were t-talking about my . . . Uncle's book which I think you will . . . find very helpful when you visit . . . Thuburbo Maius.''

"I am sure I shall," the Duke replied. "But I am saddened to hear that he is dead. Did he die out here, or was it back in England?''

"O-out . . . here," Mimosa replied.

It obviously distressed her to speak of it.

The Duke tactfully began to talk of other places he had visited and the Roman ruins he had found most interesting.

As he did so, he saw the light come back into Mimosa's eyes.

There was no mistaking the interest she was taking in what he was telling her.

It surprised him because he had never yet found a woman who was in the least concerned with his excavations, but only with himself.

Those he had talked to about them listened politely.

Then as quickly as they could they turned the conversation round to themselves, or to something more intimate.

Mimosa, however, plied him with questions about what he had found in Algeria and Libya.

Her questions were not only intelligent, he thought, but showed she had a knowledge of the subject that puzzled him.

They talked about the Romans, their history, and their enormous Empire until it was nearly time for luncheon.

"I had no idea it was so late!" Mimosa exclaimed. "Please forgive me if I have been a bore, but I found what you were telling me so absorbing.''

Before the Duke could reply, she added:

"I am sure you would like a glass of champagne. I should have suggested it sooner."

"I drink very little as a rule," the Duke admitted, "but today I feel I should celebrate your hospitality and kindness to me, and a glass of champagne would be very agreeable."

Mimosa gave the order.

As she did so, he rose to walk to the open window and look out into the garden.

"This is exactly how I thought Tunis would look," he said, "only to be disappointed when I drove from the Port through streets of dilapidated houses all in need of, if nothing else, a coat of paint."

"Some of them do look very disreputable," Mimosa agreed, "but the centre of the City has been much improved since the French arrived."

"I do not suppose the natives enjoy being made to behave themselves," the Duke remarked, "but I am sure they find eventually that it is for their own good."

Mimosa laughed.

"That sounds rather like the sort of thing my Nanny used to say to me."

"Now I come to think of it, my Nanny said the same!" the Duke replied. "So you were brought up in England?"

He was surprised that Mimosa again looked shy, and there was an obvious pause before she said:

"Both in England . . . and A-America."

He found her difficult to understand.

Considering that she had left Paris with *Comte* André, whose reputation was no secret, she seemed astonishingly unsophisticated.

In fact, she was much younger than he had expected.

"Surely you are not living here alone?" he asked.

"No . . . no," Mimosa replied. "A *Madame* Blanc, who is French, is with me, but today she has a very bad migraine and is staying in bed."

"It seemed strange that anyone as young and beautiful as yourself should not be chaperoned," the Duke remarked. "I understand you came here after your Father and Mother died in that appalling train crash. I suppose you wanted to get away from everything that reminded you of them."

"Y-yes . . . that is why I . . . came," Mimosa agreed.

She found herself tumbling over her words because she was lying.

It was bad enough pretending to be Minerva to Suzette and the servants.

She had somehow found it easier because she was speaking in a foreign language.

But to lie in English made what she said seem more of a lie, and actually more difficult to articulate.

If there was one thing her Father and Mother had always abominated, it was lies of any sort.

They had brought up Mimosa to be scrupulously truthful.

"To lie is not only cowardly," her Father had said when she was small, "it is also degrading. It humiliates you and makes you unclean in your own eyes. What is more, a lie is invariably found out.''

Now, as she lied, Mimosa hoped that the Duke would never know, and would never find her out.

She thought he seemed a kind man, and she was sure he was also very direct and truthful himself.

She was not certain how she knew this.

But she did know it, just as she had known that *Monsieur* Charlot was evil even before she learned it from his own lips.

In the same way, she was aware that the Duke was a man one could trust.

'I wonder . . . if he will . . . find me . . . out,' she thought.

She felt it would be safer to draw the conversation away from herself and talk about something else.

After luncheon the Duke said he thought he should make arrangements to reach Thuburbo Maius as soon as possible.

Mimosa told him where he could hire the best camel-drivers and added as an afterthought:

''It is, of course, better, although much more expensive, to hire horses rather than camels. As you are alone, you will not want a large tent, and they could manage a small one quite well on horseback.''

There was silence for a moment.

Then the Duke said:

''What I would really like, but I suppose I am asking for the moon, is that you should come with me. What you have said and what you have quoted from your Uncle's book tells me that I could not ask for a better Guide. And as you said, you have been there already."

Mimosa drew in her breath.

Then she knew that what the Duke had suggested was something she would very much like to do.

It would give her a chance to see her Father's grave again and to pray at it.

She also wanted to see the Duke's reaction to Thuburbo Maius.

Would it thrill him as it had thrilled her and her Father?

But she told herself that of course such an idea was impossible.

Then she asked herself:

"Why is it impossible?"

She was her own mistress, beholden to no-one.

Who would know or care whether she went to Thuburbo Maius or stayed in the Villa listening to Suzette?

The Duke was watching her until she said:

"If you ... really think I w-would be of ... help ... then of course ... I would ... like to ... go with you to Thuburbo Maius."

He clapped his hands together.

"Wonderful!" he exclaimed. "Thank you, thank you! I know you can help me, and I am more grateful than I can possibly say."

"Of one thing I must warn you—you must be very careful of the snakes. My ... my Uncle ... died from a ... snake-bite."

"You were with him at the time?"

The question caught her off-guard.

For a moment she could see her Father's face after the snake had bitten him.

She saw again the effort he had made to walk back towards the tents before he had collapsed onto the ground.

"Y-yes . . . I was . . . there," she said in a voice barely above a whisper.

"It must have been very upsetting for you," the Duke remarked, "and perhaps it is cruel of me to ask you to return."

"No, no! I want to . . . go back," Mimosa said firmly, as if she had suddenly made up her mind. "I want . . . to see . . . his grave."

"You mean—he is buried there?" the Duke asked incredulously.

"The men who were with us were afraid to touch him. They are very superstitious and believe the snakes are the protectors of the sacred Temples, and that is why they bite intruders."

"Then I must be careful not to violate their privacy," the Duke said. "But I imagine it is something which does not happen very often."

"It used to be scorpions of which we had to be careful in other parts of the world," Mimosa remarked.

The Duke said nothing.

He noticed it was the first time she had spoken of having been to other Roman ruins.

He had thought she had only read about the sites in Libya and Algeria of which he had been talking.

Then he told himself it was impossible.

What he had heard of Tison had connected him not with the Cities of the past, but only the Cities of the present.

His journeys to and from America were frequently reported in the English newspapers.

The Duke remembered reading that he had interests in practically every country in Europe.

Because he was so rich, there were innumerable articles written about him.

The Press followed and fêted him as if he were Royalty.

But the Duke could never remember reading of his visiting the places that he had been discussing with Tison's daughter.

On the other hand, it was obvious from their conversation that she had as intimate a knowledge of some of the Roman Cities as he had himself.

He remembered quite distinctly *Comte* André telling him that he himself had never visited Thuburbo Maius.

In that case, why, he wondered, was Tison's daughter there with her Uncle?

Surely Sir Richard could not have approved of her love-affair with the *Comte*.

It all flashed through the Duke's mind.

But he was careful to say nothing of it to Mimosa, as he was afraid of upsetting her.

Taking her advice, he went to the place where he could obtain the best horses to take with him on his expedition.

Because of his title and his authoritative air, he was able to obtain the best service, also a promise that they would be ready to set out the following morning.

When he returned to the Villa it was time to dress for dinner.

He appreciated the comfort of his bedroom, where Jenkins was waiting for him.

"It's fine 'ere, Your Grace," Jenkins said. "Good food an' beds like you was sleepin' on a cloud!"

The Duke smiled.

"Then I will leave you to enjoy it," he said, "while I go off with a caravan tomorrow."

"Suits me, Your Grace. I can do wi'out lyin' on the hard ground an' all that rubble."

The Duke laughed.

He was used to Jenkins expressing himself firmly on the subject of his excavations.

The Duke, however, appreciated the delicious dinner he enjoyed with Mimosa.

She was looking exceedingly lovely in a gown that had belonged to her Cousin.

It had obviously been designed in Paris.

She was slimmer than Minerva, but she was aware that the servants and Suzette assumed it was because she had been half-starved by her kidnappers.

She found it exciting to be going downstairs to dine alone with a man.

She suspected that her Mother would not have approved of her going alone with him to Thuburbo Maius.

However, she felt certain her Father would understand.

The least she could do would be to show him the

beauty of the Roman ruins.

Perhaps he would go back to England with a greater appreciation of them than he had had before.

"If I question him," she said to herself, "without his being aware of what I am doing, perhaps he will help me to make up my mind as to what I should do and where I should go."

It was all rather vague.

Yet she felt that the mere fact that the Duke was there had helped her already.

She was no longer as frightened as she had been.

After dinner they went into the Sitting-Room, where the windows were still open into the garden.

Mimosa walked out onto the green lawn followed by the Duke.

She looked up at the stars, feeling that soon she would see them again over Thuburbo Maius.

She remembered that was how she had seen them with her Father in an isolated spot where there was no other human habitation.

Although she was unaware of it, the Duke was watching her.

After a moment he asked:

"Surely you are very lonely here now that *Comte* André has left? What do you intend to do with yourself?"

"I will go to England," Mimosa replied.

"In the meantime you are alone and wasting your beauty," the Duke persisted. "You are very lovely, Miss Tison, as a great number of people must have told you."

Mimosa was looking at the stars and shook her head.

"Nobody has ever said that to me," she replied, "but . . . I hope it is . . . true."

The Duke did not speak.

He wondered why she bothered to lie.

Did she really think he was unaware that *Comte* André had been her lover?

That they had been here alone together until he had had to return to Paris?

Jenkins had told him that Miss Tison had been broken-hearted when the *Comte* left her.

Also that she had been kidnapped by a gang of criminals and had returned only a few days before, having completely lost her memory.

The Duke had been astounded and found it hard to believe.

Jenkins had questioned the Chef, who spoke English.

It was confirmed by the man-servant who had actually been engaged by the *Comte* with all the other servants.

"She is not only a liar," the Duke told himself "she is also a very good actress!"

He thought Mimosa's impersonation of a young girl who knew little of the Social World, and certainly nothing of men, was fantastic.

But how, he asked himself, could she make herself blush to order?

How could she manage to look so shy and appear so ingenuous when he paid her a compliment.

He chided himself.

He should be content with what the Gods had sent him, which was exactly what he wanted: a Guide to Thuburbo Maius.

If Miss Tison wanted to pretend that she was pure and innocent, why should he challenge her?

She was giving him a comfortable bed in a very attractive Villa.

She had also promised to be his Guide to Thuburbo Maius.

It was ungrateful to ask for more.

But he knew as they turned back to go into the house that he was more than ordinarily curious. In fact, he was definitely intrigued.

On the table in the Sitting-Room was Sir Richard's manuscript, and Mimosa said:

"I feel sure you will want to read as much as you can tonight before you go to sleep, but I would rather you did not take it with you tomorrow."

"If you are offering me an excuse to come back here after I have made my explorations," the Duke asked, "then I accept most gratefully."

"I could not . . . bear anything to . . . happen to . . . it," Mimosa said.

"I promise you that as far as I am concerned, I will be extremely careful. However, I agree with you that it would be unsafe to take it with us in case the ground is damp or it becomes covered in dust, as sometimes happens. At least in Africa, if nowhere else!"

"I know that," Mimosa said. "Once we encountered a cloud of locusts, which was more frightening than any sand-storm."

She was remembering how they had been riding across some very barren land, when the camel-drivers had pointed ahead.

She had seen what had looked like a dark cloud low in the clear sky.

The men leapt from their camels and her Father did the same from his horse.

Mimosa followed their example.

The camel-drivers ordered the camels to kneel down so that they could shelter behind them.

The locusts had flown over them and they had heard their wings beating overhead.

Only when there was no further sound had Mimosa opened her eyes.

Some of the locusts had attached themselves to her horse and there were one or two on her shoulders.

The camel-drivers were killing them or brushing them away so that they flew off to catch up with the rest.

It had been a frightening experience.

Mimosa had no idea that what she said made the Duke even more curious than he was already.

Then she looked at the clock.

"If we are to leave early," she said, "I think it would be wise to go to bed."

"I agree with you," he answered.

She walked towards the door which he opened for her and they walked up the attractive staircase side by side.

When they reached the landing on which both

their bedrooms were situated, Mimosa held out her hand.

"Goodnight, Your Grace," she said. "I have enjoyed our conversation more than I can possibly say. I only hope that what you see when you get to Thuburbo Maius will be included in your book."

"I doubt if I can write as well as your Uncle," the Duke said as he smiled, "but with your help I have a feeling I shall miss nothing which is of real interest."

"Now you are flattering me," Mimosa said, "and I shall feel responsible if later Archaeologists think you were very remiss for passing by something important."

The Duke laughed.

"We must ask the Gods to protect us."

"I hope you have everything you need," Mimosa said politely.

She put out her hand and he took it, wondering if he should kiss it, or perhaps kiss her.

As the *Comte* had been her lover, she must think him very slow for not making advances towards her.

Surely any woman living alone, as she was, in this exquisitely beautiful Villa, would expect every man who visited her to beg for her favours?

It all flashed through the Duke's mind.

Then Mimosa took her hand from his and walked towards her bedroom door.

"Goodnight, Your Grace, and God Bless you," she said.

It was something she had always said to her Father, and now it came automatically to her lips.

Having reached her bedroom, she went in and shut the door behind her.

It left the Duke staring at the closed door with a puzzled expression on his face.

Was it possible, he asked himself, that for the first time in his life a beautiful woman had left him without looking back with an unmistakable invitation in her eyes?

Certainly no woman, with the exception of his Mother, had ever called down the Blessing of God as she left him.

The women he knew invariably suggested that they themselves might be the blessing he required.

The Duke went into his bedroom and shut the door.

He was quite certain something strange and unsual was happening!

Yet he could not imagine what it was.

Then his perception, or what he thought of as his instinct, told him that what had at first seemed straight-forward was something very different.

The difference was, he had to admit, that Miss Tison was one of the most intelligent young women he had ever met.

As he got into bed he thought of the conversation they had at dinner.

It astounded him.

chapter six

MIMOSA felt elated from the moment she awoke next morning.

It was very early, but she got up and dressed.

She packed the few things she thought she would want while she was away at Thuburbo Maius.

When she came downstairs she was not surprised to find that the Duke was already having breakfast.

He rose as she entered the room.

Then, as she sat down and Jacques hurried to bring her dishes from the kitchen, he said:

"You are quite certain this is not going to be too arduous for you?"

The way he spoke told Mimosa without words that he had learnt from somebody that she had been kidnapped

This was not surprising, but at the same time she

felt embarrassed because she was now acting another lie.

The Duke, in fact, was being very careful not to remind her of what had happened to her.

He knew that when people lost their memory they should be left in peace until they could recall everything for themselves.

He therefore accepted Mimosa's assurance that she would be all right and talked of other things.

Jacques drove them into the City in a comfortable carriage.

The Duke guessed it had been bought by *Comte* André.

They went to the place where their caravan was waiting.

Mimosa saw at once that the horses were young and fresh.

She knew they would travel a great deal more swiftly than if they had hired camels.

Her suitcase was strapped on one side of the saddle of one horse and the Duke's on the other side.

Before she left the Villa, Mimosa had asked after *Madame* Blanc, only to be told that she had not yet been called.

She could not help feeling a sense of relief.

She had no wish to go into long explanations as to where she was going and why.

The servants knew, of course, and she thought that Suzette would be curious enough on her return, especially when she learnt she was accompanied by a Duke.

It was not yet hot, although it was well after sunrise.

As they rode out of the City, Mimosa eagerly pointed out to the Duke what was left of Hadrian's tremendous Aqueduct.

It had been built by the Emperor to bring pure water from the mountains the eighty miles to Carthage.

It was amazing that it was still standing.

The Duke was as impressed as Mimosa had been when she had first seen it.

"The water passes through the hills by means of an underground canal," Mimosa explained, "and the Roman canals are still used in some parts of the City."

The Duke thought it extraordinary.

What he found even more extraordinary was the light shining in Mimosa's eyes.

He was also impressed by the way she rode her obstreperous horse.

He realised without asking questions that she must be used to riding.

He wondered if it had been on her Father's Ranch in America.

Alternatively, he mused, it might have been on the "broad acres" of the hunting-fields in England.

As they rode on their way, Mimosa pointed out various Roman pillars and the "Temple of the Nymphs" built in the 2nd century.

The Duke became more and more intrigued.

It was certainly unusual that a young woman who ought to be listening to the compliments paid to her by men should be so thrilled by what had been built centuries in the past.

They stopped for luncheon under some shady trees with the view stretching away to the horizon.

They ate the delicious food which had been prepared by the Chef at the Villa.

"This is such a lovely country!" Mimosa said as she looked at the view.

"And therefore very appropriate to you," the Duke remarked. "At the same time, surely, you find it very lonely without somebody with you?"

He thought perhaps he was speaking out of turn, but Mimosa answered dreamily:

"I have . . . not been . . . alone . . . for long."

He assumed she was referring to the *Comte*.

It suddenly annoyed him that anyone so beautiful and apparently unspoilt should be yearning for a man who was notorious for his many passionate affairs.

Rising to his feet, the Duke said somewhat sharply: "I think we should go!"

The way he spoke made Mimosa look at him in surprise.

She wondered what had upset him.

Then she told herself she was being selfish.

She was dilly-dallying when he was so eager to get to Thuburbo Maius.

They rode on and stopped only when the horses were growing tired.

It was important that their tents should be erected and they should have something to eat before the sun sank and it grew dark.

Mimosa chose a perfect place to encamp, sloping down to a small lake.

There was a level piece of ground on which to erect their tents.

She noticed there was a large one and a small one.

The men were putting them up a little apart from each other.

The Duke was also looking in the same direction, and he asked unexpectedly:

"You will not be nervous sleeping by yourself? Would you rather we shared the large tent together?"

Mimosa appeared not to realize there was anything significant in the question.

She merely answered:

"I think I should feel safer if my tent were nearer yours."

It was not what the Duke had actually suggested.

He smiled cynically as she told the men to move the smaller tent closer to the other one.

He could not help wondering if she was playing "hard to get," or if in fact she was not at all aware of him as a man.

He thought mockingly that the latter explanation was very good for his ego.

It was certainly unusual not to have a woman ready to fall into his arms almost before he asked her name.

He had grown so used to being pursued in London, and especially stalked by Lady Sybil.

It was impossible for him not to wonder what was in Mimosa's mind.

She came back to his side to say:

"As soon as the tents are erected, I think I will go to bed. We should leave early, and as we have only about ten miles left to go, it should not take us long to reach Thuburbo Maius."

"That sounds like an excellent suggestion," the Duke agreed, "and, of course, you must take the larger tent."

Mimosa laughed.

"Because I am the larger person?"

"I am not saying that!"

"The big tent is for you," she insisted, "and the little one is for me. It is everything I need and, if I am frightened, I can call out and you will hear me."

As she spoke she was thinking of how Minerva had been abducted, not from a tent miles away from human habitation, but from her own garden.

The expression in her eyes made the Duke say quickly:

"If you are feeling at all frightened, I have just told you that you can sleep in my tent and I will protect you."

"That you will be near me is very reassuring," Mimosa answered. "Goodnight, and thank you for a wonderful day."

She went into the small tent, and the Duke went into his.

However, thinking about her, it took him a long time to get to sleep.

The next morning they set off as soon as their horses were saddled and the tents packed on the backs of the other horses.

Mimosa was looking ahead of her.

When she saw ahead of her, silhouetted against the sky in the far distance, the tall pillars of Jupiter's Temple, she felt excited.

At the same time, her whole being cried out for her Father.

How could he have left her so suddenly?

How could the most exciting excursion they had ever undertaken end so dismally?

With difficulty she forced back the tears, afraid that the Duke would see them and ask uncomfortable questions.

Mimosa knew he kept glancing at her, but he said nothing.

When finally they reached Thuburbo Maius, Mimosa led the way to what she knew was a good place to pitch their camp.

It was below the hill on which the City had been built.

There were a number of shrubs as well as trees, which would give some protection against the sun.

They left their horses with the men and started to walk up the easy slope.

Mimosa had not put on that morning her riding-skirt and the thin muslin blouse she had worn when they left Tunis.

Instead, she put on a gown of blue muslin which accentuated the blue of her eyes and the gold of her hair.

It was a very pretty gown and certainly one she would not usually have worn to go riding.

But she knew that if she waited until she arrived

to change, it would delay the moment that the Duke was longing for.

That was to see Jupiter's Temple in Thuburbo Maius.

It was one building that had been completely excavated.

Most of the area around it on which the City had been built was still waiting to be cleared.

As they reached the top of the hill, the Temple was in sight just to their left.

Mimosa stood still so that she could watch the expression on the Duke's face.

The Temple was certainly impressive.

Four columns were still standing, with their Corinthian capitals, facing the monumental staircase.

They had originally supported a frieze and the cornice of the triangular pediment at the end of the building.

There were also the truncated remains of six other columns standing, whose capitals lay scattered on the floor.

Of the twenty-two steps of the great staircase leading up to the base on which the Temple had stood, thirteen were in fairly good condition, and part of the Forum had been cleared.

It was therefore easy to see how impressive it had looked when it had towered over the whole City.

"It is fantastic!" the Duke exclaimed, and knew how delighted Mimosa was at his appreciation.

She led him to the steps of the Temple, which had been the religious and political centre of the Town.

It was there that official religious ceremonies took

place and, as in most Roman Cities, the planners arranged for the Capitol to dominate the Forum.

The Forum stretched out some distance, and Mimosa told the Duke what her Father had told her: that beyond it was the market-place.

It was a small square with a well in the centre.

Beyond it were many houses, still covered by the debris of centuries.

One could only imagine, therefore, what they had looked like when they were filled with busy people, tradesmen, shopkeepers, farmers, government officials, and everyone else who lived in the City.

Not far from the Temple, and surprisingly recognisable, were the remains of two large buildings which had housed, Mimosa told the Duke, the Baths. One was a Winter Bath, the other a Summer Bath.

The Duke was delighted with them and spent some time in both buildings.

"I only hope I can come back," he said, "when these places have all been properly excavated. I am sure there is a great deal more to be discovered than we can even begin to imagine!"

"That is what . . . my Uncle has said in his book," Mimosa answered.

Then she went on:

"There are also some chambers beneath the Temple, but I have not seen them."

"We will have plenty of time to see them later," the Duke said. "I think now we should go back and have something to eat."

"Now that you mention it, I am rather hungry," Mimosa agreed.

Their attendants had spread a picnic for them beneath the trees.

The Chef had made sure they would not go hungry.

"I suppose tonight," the Duke remarked, "we shall have to trust ourselves to the cooking of our attendants, but I have an idea it will not be very palatable."

"I am sure we shall have enough food," Mimosa answered. "The Chef assured me that he was used to providing for people who did long journeys to look at the ruins, and therefore knew exactly what was needed."

The Duke smiled at her.

"I know that I am very lucky," he said, "to have you not only as my Guide, but also as my hostess. You think of everything, which I can imagine no-one else doing."

He thought of how helpless Lady Sybil would have been in such a situation.

On none of his expeditions had he ever taken a woman with him, because he knew they would be more of an encumbrance than a help.

Miss Tison was certainly different.

He thought it must be her American upbringing which made her so practical.

After luncheon they hurried back to the ruins of the City, where the Duke wandered about trying to imagine how it had looked when it was first built.

Mimosa sat down on what was left of the wall of a house and watched him.

She knew his imagination was working, just as her Father's had.

He had stepped back over the centuries and was living in A.D. 168 when the twenty-foot columns of the Temple were first raised.

She tried to imagine the Romans moving about the City when it was revived after a period of decline in the 4th century by Constantine II, son of Constantine the Great.

Mimosa remembered her Father telling her how it later fell victim to the Vandals and was abandoned in later Byzantine times.

"It has experienced misery, joy, and despair," she told herself, "which I suppose is true of most human beings."

She knew for the moment she was happy because she was with the Duke and did not have to worry about the future.

What she had felt until his appearance was a dark cloud looming nearer and nearer.

'When he leaves,' she thought, 'I shall make up my mind what to do . . . perhaps go to England . . . alone."

However sensible she tried to be, she knew the idea was very frightening.

It was with difficulty that she prevented herself from jumping up and running to his side.

She wanted to feel again the sense of security she had known last night.

She had been alone in her small tent, listening to him moving about as he prepared for sleep.

The air was very still, and she had wondered if

he would be shocked if she went into his tent and talked to him in the darkness.

She thought if they could not see each other she might find it easier to tell him the truth about herself and ask his advice.

Then she knew it was a shocking idea to think of going into what was in effect a man's bedroom when he was trying to sleep.

He would not understand it was only because she wanted to talk to him in the dark.

She knew she would find it very difficult in the light, for she would be afraid of the condemnation she would see in his eyes.

He would be shocked that she had professed to be her Cousin and had deceived the servants at the Villa.

There was also the problem, and she had not forgotten it, of *Monsieur* Charlot.

He had said he would return within a week.

By that time she would be back at the Villa and perhaps the Duke would have gone.

"Shall I tell him, or would it be a mistake?" Mimosa wondered.

Now her eyes were on the Duke as he bent to pick up something from the ground.

He beckoned to her and, because it was anyway what she wanted to do, she hurried towards him.

"What is it?" she asked.

"I have a *souvenir* for you," he explained.

He put a small coin into her hand.

She realised it was a coin that had been in circulation many hundreds of years ago, when the City was prosperous.

"I shall keep it for luck," Mimosa said.

"That is what it will bring you," the Duke replied, "in fact, everything you wish for yourself."

Mimosa gave a little sigh.

"The difficulty is," she said, "I am not quite certain what I do wish."

"Then you are different from most women!" he said.

She looked at him enquiringly, and he explained:

"Most women want a husband to protect them, and children who are a part of themselves."

"Yes, that is what I want," Mimosa said a little dreamily, "although of course it depends on who the husband would be."

"Naturally," the Duke agreed a little dryly.

He thought now was the moment he had been expecting for some time, when she would look at him with that invitational look in her eyes that he knew so well.

Instead of which, she looked at the Temple and said:

"While I am here I shall say a prayer to Jupiter and hope he will give me what I want."

"And of course I shall add my prayers to yours," the Duke replied.

"Are you going to ask him to find you a wife," Mimosa enquired.

The Duke shook his head.

"I am very happy as a bachelor."

"You must be very careful," Mimosa said, "and when you do marry, find somebody you love so much that you know it would not be worth living without her."

She was thinking of her Father and Mother and how blissfully happy they had been.

There was a little break in her voice and a hint of tears in her eyes.

The Duke assumed she was thinking of *Comte* André and how badly he had behaved towards her.

It annoyed him so much that he walked away without another word.

Mimosa sat down on the nearest pile of rubble and thought of her Father and Mother.

She had not yet gone to her Father's grave.

She had promised herself she would go there in the late afternoon, just as the sun was sinking.

It was only a little way from where they were camped, and she wanted to be there alone.

She was deep in her thoughts when the Duke came back to her side.

"I think you must be hungry," he said, "and we should go back to camp and have something to eat before it gets dark."

"I am sure that is a sensible idea," Mimosa said.

She had been so intent on her thoughts that she had not realised that the sun had lost its strength.

Now it was sinking low over the horizon.

The sky was still clear, but she knew that darkness, when it came, came swiftly.

It would be a mistake, she knew, not to leave

while the way was clear amongst the ruins of the houses.

There was also the occasional ditch into which one could fall if one were not careful.

She walked towards the Forum, then stood for a moment, looking up at the majesty of the Temple.

As she did so, the Duke joined her, saying:

"I am sure if you pray here for what you want, your prayer will be heard."

Even as he spoke, from one side of the Capitol some men appeared.

It was so unexpected, since there had been no-one about all day, that Mimosa stared at them in astonishment.

Then she gave a sudden scream.

She was seized by one of the men and, before she could realise what was happening, he had picked her up in his arms.

As he did so, she was aware that three other men had closed in on the Duke.

He was fighting frantically, but was being overpowered.

She tried to free herself, but she was helpless in her captor's strong arms.

He carried her down the side of the Capitol.

Her screams seemed lost against the vastness of the wall they were passing with the pillars towering above them.

Now she saw that one man was running ahead.

He opened what appeared to be a door in the back of the base of the Capitol.

The man who carried her flung her inside, and she fell to the ground.

Even as she did so, she was joined by the Duke.

He was thrown down in the same way by the three men who carried him.

The heavy door was slammed shut behind them, and there was the sound of a bar being put across it.

As they did so, Mimosa heard one man say in Arabic:

"Now go and fetch the Master."

Then there was the sound of their footsteps walking away, followed by silence.

The Duke managed to get to his feet, and he bent down and pulled Mimosa to hers.

She gave a little gasp.

"I . . . I think they have . . . kidnapped us!" she murmured.

She was thinking as she spoke that this was what must have happened to Minerva.

Perhaps they too would just disappear as she had.

The Duke put his arms around her and said in a deliberately quiet voice:

"I suppose they are holding us for ransom."

Mimosa drew in her breath.

Then she managed to say:

"I heard one of them say as they shut the door:

" 'Go and fetch the Master.' "

"Then the whole thing is a well-thought-out plot," the Duke said. "I imagine these scoundrels intend to demand a large ransom because they think whatever they ask you will be able to pay."

"Th-they may . . . kill us!" Mimosa answered in a frightened voice.

"I think that is unlikely, for then they would get no money," the Duke said. "This is my fault! I should never have brought you here. I have heard before how these criminals work, following someone whom they think is rich until the opportunity comes to kidnap them and demand a huge ransom to set them free."

His voice was harsh as he asked:

"How can I have been such a fool as to come here without bringing a revolver?"

Mimosa, who was standing close to him with her head resting on his shoulder, gave a scream.

"What is it?" he asked.

"Snakes!" she exclaimed. "There are . . . snakes in . . . here and they may . . . bite us!"

She knew when the Duke did not answer that he had already thought of that possibility.

They were in darkness except for a few chinks of light coming from places in the wall where the stone-work had been damaged.

There was also a hole in the roof from which tiles had fallen.

"It is . . . dangerous! I know . . . it is . . . dangerous!" Mimosa exclaimed.

The Duke looked around him as if trying to find something on which they could sit.

It was then Mimosa gave another cry.

"Papa told me," she said, "that there are steps by which the Priests . . . climbed up from below onto the platform of the Temple."

The Duke understood.

He picked up Mimosa in his arms and walked to a corner of the chamber.

She could just make out in the dim light that there were the remains of what had been steps rising up to the roof.

The Duke put her down, and she said, looking up:

"I can see at . . . the top there is . . . a hole that must have been . . . a way out. I will . . . climb up and . . . look."

"You had better let me do that," the Duke suggested.

As he spoke, a piece of masonry came away under Mimosa's hand.

"I am lighter than you," she said, "and the steps are . . . crumbling away. Let me . . . go first."

She could feel rather than see her way.

She climbed very slowly while the Duke stood below, ready to catch her if she fell.

Small pieces of stone from the steps broke away and dropped down, but she reached the top safely.

There had been, she saw, quite a large aperture at one time.

However, one of the Corinthian capitals had fallen from its pillar half-way across it.

It gave her something to hold on to, and she looked out cautiously.

She realised how high she was above the Forum.

It was then she saw sitting on the bottom steps of the great staircase leading up to the Temple four of the men who had abducted them.

She guessed that the fifth had gone in search of the "master," whoever he might be.

They had built themselves a small fire and were now preparing something to eat.

Mimosa thought the light from the flames was comforting to them now that it was only a short time before dusk.

It was then she had an idea.

She crept slowly backwards and began the descent back into the chamber.

As soon as she reached him, the Duke lifted her down so that now she was beside him.

"What is happening?" he asked.

"Four of the men are preparing food for themselves at the bottom of the staircase and the other has gone to fetch the 'Master.' But I have an idea! I know how superstitious the Tunisians are, and they are well aware that this is a . . . sacred place."

"What do you intend to do?" the Duke asked.

"I am going to try to frighten them," she answered.

As she spoke, she began to undo her gown, which she fastened down the front.

The Duke could hardly see her in the darkness.

But he was aware of what she was doing and waited in surprise until she slipped her gown off completely.

Underneath it she was wearing a stiff white bust-bodice.

It fitted closely over a tightly-laced corset such as was worn by every woman.

Beneath the full skirt of her gown she had on a white satin petticoat.

It had belonged to Minerva, and was trimmed with rows of lace.

The important thing for Mimosa's plan was that all her clothing now was white.

She released the pins from her hair so that it fell down her back.

"Follow me up if you can," she said, "but join me only if they run away. Otherwise I will come back for you."

"For God's sake," the Duke urged, "take care of yourself! I feel I am wrong in letting you do this. If only I had a weapon of some sort!"

"I shall be . . . all right," Mimosa said, "and perhaps I can save . . . both of us."

She looked up at him.

For one moment he could see by the now-faint light coming through a chink in the masonry that her eyes were pleading with him.

She was begging him to understand and her lips were close to his.

Instinctively, the Duke put his arms round her, bent his head, and kissed her.

For a moment Mimosa was completely still in astonishment.

Then, as his lips took possession of hers, she felt as if she melted into him.

There was a sudden streak of ecstasy in her breast that she had never felt before.

Everything else was forgotten.

That they were prisoners, that there were men outside who menaced them.

That there were snakes that might destroy them.

All she could think of was the wonder of the Duke's kiss.

She had never thought of it before, but suddenly she knew she loved him.

The Duke raised his head.

Without thinking, Mimosa whispered:

"I . . . always thought a . . . kiss would be . . . as wonderful as that!"

Then she turned and started to climb again up the steps.

The Duke followed her as she disappeared round the fallen Corinthian capital onto the platform above the steps.

For a moment she stood there.

Then, as the men below were suddenly aware of her, they turned their heads.

Mimosa raised her arms.

Speaking in Arabic, she said:

"This is the sacred Temple of Jupiter, King of the Gods! You trespass here and insult his dignity and his holiness by your presence and the evil you are planning. He sends me as his messenger to curse you, your wives, and your children now and for all future generations. The wrath of the Lord Jupiter will pursue you, and you will never be free of this curse in punishment for what you have done and what you plan to do!"

Her voice rang out and seemed to echo over the abandoned City.

Pointing down to the men, she went on:

"Go! Go now, before he destroys you and you lie dead here in the place that is sacred to the great God!"

Before she could finish the last words, the four men had all jumped up and were running as fast as they could go.

There was no doubt that they were terror-struck.

They stumbled over the broken stones and debris until they disappeared.

Only their small fire remained, flickering in a faint breeze that had sprung up.

Mimosa gave a little sigh as the Duke joined her.

"You were marvellous, absolutely magnificent!" he said. "Come, let us get away from here as quickly as we can!"

He led the way down the great steps from the platform to ground level, stopping at the bottom only to pick up a gun.

It had been left behind by one of their kidnappers in his haste to get away.

They turned towards the path by which they had come.

As they did so, a man came riding up on horseback.

He was a large man.

As Mimosa looked at him, hoping he was somebody who had come to help them, she saw that he had a black mask over his face.

It reminded her of the Highwaymen in England who used to hold up rich travellers on the road.

When he saw the Duke and Mimosa, he drew in his horse.

"Stop!" he commanded. "Stop or I will kill you!"

He pulled a revolver from his belt as he spoke.

Before he had got it completely free, however, the Duke fired the gun he had picked up near the fire.

He was not even sure it was loaded, but it was, and the Duke was a very good shot.

The man on the horse received the bullet right through his heart.

With an unpleasant sound he dropped his revolver and fell from his horse to the ground.

It had all happened almost instantaneously.

Mimosa could only stand paralysed by the shock and horror of it.

Then the Duke reached out and took her hand.

"Hurry!" he said. "It would be a mistake to linger here in case the other men come back."

He spoke calmly, and somehow it helped her to think clearly.

Because they were taking the same path by which the man on the horse had come up, they had to pass close to him.

He was lying on the ground, while his horse had moved away.

His hat had fallen off and his mask had dropped below his chin.

As Mimosa took a quick look at him, she knew who he was.

Monsieur Charlot.

The Duke did not stop, but walked quickly down

the incline towards their camp.

He was relieved to see when they reached it that the horses were there.

But there was no sign of their attendants.

"They have run away!" the Duke said. "Or else they were in league with those wretches who tried to kidnap us!"

"What . . . shall we . . . do?" Mimosa asked.

"Leave as quickly as we can," the Duke answered sharply.

The horses had been unsaddled and their bridles removed.

But their legs had been hobbled so that they could not go far.

They were cropping what little grass there was.

The Duke found the saddles where they had been placed nearby.

He put one on the horse that Mimosa had ridden.

Quickly she went inside the tent she had used the night before.

She put on the white blouse and her riding-skirt in which she had travelled the day before.

It took her only a few minutes, but by the time she went back to the Duke her horse was saddled and bridled.

He was now coping with his own horse.

He stopped for a moment to lift Mimosa onto her saddle.

Then he released the ropes round the horses' legs.

In only a very few minutes they were riding away from the camp.

There was still no sign of their attendants.

They had ridden for nearly an hour before Mimosa drew in her horse and said to the Duke:

"What about the men we employed? Will they be all right?"

"They can look after themselves," he answered. "They should have protected us from those criminals, and I intend when we reach Tunis to report them for negligence. At the same time, I shall report the death of the man I killed."

Mimosa was silent for a moment.

Then she said in a small voice:

"I . . . I know . . . who he . . . is."

The Duke looked at her in surprise.

"You recognised him?"

Mimosa nodded.

"He is . . . a *Monsieur* Charlot."

"How is it that you know him?"

"H-he . . . was . . . trying to . . . blackmail me!"

The Duke was so astonished that for a moment he did not speak.

Then he asked:

"Blackmail you? For what?"

Too late Mimosa wished she had not admitted knowing the dead man.

It had been such a shock.

She had forgotten that the Duke should not know about him, or what he was threatening to reveal to the *Comte*'s wife.

"That I . . . cannot tell . . . you," she said after a moment.

The Duke smiled reassuringly at her.

"It is of no importance," he said, "and we will

talk about it later. All that matters now is that we should get back safely, and that matters very much indeed.''

He put out his hand as he spoke, and Mimosa, riding beside him, gave him hers.

She found the hard pressure of his fingers very comforting.

''Let me tell you,'' the Duke said quietly, ''that I think you are utterly and completely magnificent! No other woman could have been as brave or wonderful as you!''

Mimosa blushed.

They rode fast and in silence.

The daylight was by now fading fast, but she knew the Duke was eager to get her away from danger.

'I love him!' she thought. 'I love him . . . but he must . . . never know it!'

chapter seven

THEY rode until the Duke was aware that Mimosa was exhausted.

She was very pale and he thought she was swaying in the saddle.

It was then, at the end of a village, he saw a Mosque.

It was only a very small one, but he drew up outside it and gave Mimosa his reins to hold.

By this time the stars were fading and it would be only a little while before the dawn broke.

The Duke fortunately saw a man coming out of a cottage on his way to work.

He spoke to him and asked where the Imam of the Mosque lived.

The man pointed to a house just a short distance away from the Mosque.

The Duke walked to the door, and after he had knocked on it for some minutes it was opened by an elderly man.

He had obviously been awoken by the noise.

The Duke explained in a mixture of Arabic, in which he was not as fluent as Mimosa, and French what he required.

He also explained how they were hurrying away from Thuburbo Maius because they had been attacked by robbers.

The Imam made an exclamation of disgust and told him that he could bring his wife into the house.

The Duke had realised that all Moslems were very particular about the purity of their women.

The Imam would be shocked at the idea of his travelling alone with a young woman to whom he was not married.

He therefore had made it quite clear that it was his wife for whom he was concerned.

He hurried back to where Mimosa was holding the horses.

As he reached her, he noticed a boy of about fifteen standing watching them.

He beckoned to him, and when he came told him to hold the horses.

The Duke then lifted Mimosa down from the saddle.

He did not put her on the ground because he was sure she was incapable of walking.

Instead, he carried her into the house where the Imam was waiting at the door.

They were led into a room which was small and obviously kept for guests.

It was sparsely furnished.

There was a divan raised about six inches from the floor on which lay several cushions.

There was also a praying-mat and one chair.

The Duke put Mimosa gently down on the divan.

As he did so, he said softly in English:

"I must go to see to the horses. If the Imam should speak to you, I have told him you are my wife."

He saw Mimosa's eyes widen.

Then he hurried from the room and was relieved because the Imam followed him.

When they reached the door, the Imam told him there was a stable at the back of the house.

The Duke found the stable and put the horses into two empty stalls.

He took off their saddles and bridles with the help of the boy, whom he tipped and thanked.

It all took a little time.

He went back to the house and found that the door was ajar.

The Imam was nowhere to be seen and he assumed he must have gone back to bed.

The Duke went back into the room where he had left Mimosa.

He was not surprised to find her fast asleep.

The Imam had left a candle burning on the table.

By the light of it the Duke could see she had turned her face, like a child, against the pillow.

Her hands were tucked under her cheek.

She looked very lovely, very young, and very innocent.

The Duke stood looking at her for quite some time.

He gently took off her shoes.

He then removed his boots and lay down on the divan beside her.

She did not stir, and he realised she was sleeping the sleep of utter exhaustion.

He was aware that what she had done to disturb and terrify the kidnappers must have cost her a tremendous effort.

At the same time, she had been very frightened in case she was not successful, and instead of running away, they attacked her.

The Duke blew out the candle.

There was a slight twist to his lips as he did so.

He was thinking that, if his friends were told he was lying beside the most beautiful girl he had ever seen without touching her, they would not believe it.

Resolutely the Duke forced himself to make his mind a blank and try to sleep.

Mimosa awoke with a start.

As the sun was pouring through the window, she knew it was late in the morning.

For a moment she could not think where she was.

As she looked round the small room, the memory of what had happened the day before came flooding back to her.

The last thing she remembered was the Duke carrying her into the house.

She wondered where he was now.

She turned over and was suddenly aware that the other half of the divan on which she had slept was ruffled and there was an indentation in a cushion beside her head.

Had he really slept beside her, she wondered, and blushed at the thought.

It seemed impossible.

And yet everything that had happened since she came to Tunis had been incredible!

She sat up and saw her shoes put neatly together on the floor.

She knew the Duke must have removed them for her.

She was blushing again as she got up.

There was a mirror on the wall hanging between two pictures.

She looked into it and was horrified at the untidiness of her hair.

She tried to smooth it into place and to fasten it with the few pins she had left.

She opened the door of the room, hoping to find somewhere to wash.

It was not difficult, for almost next door was a sink with a large jug standing in it filled with water.

She washed her face and hands and found a towel with which to dry herself.

Then she decided to explore further.

She had not far to go.

Just across the narrow hall she could hear voices.

When she opened the door she found the Duke and the Imam sitting at a table having a meal.

They rose as she entered.

The Imam said in French:

"*Bonjour, Mademoiselle*, I hope you have slept well."

"I am very grateful to you," Mimosa replied. "I was so tired, I do not think I could have gone another inch further!"

The Imam smiled and pulled out a chair for her to sit.

"Have something to eat," the Duke said. "His Reverence is exceedingly kind in allowing us to join him at his midday meal."

Mimosa was hungry.

She enjoyed the yoghurt which she knew was served in every Tunisian house.

She also enjoyed the typical native dish which followed it.

It was accompanied by mint tea, the national beverage in all Arab countries.

She realised the Duke was in a hurry to be leaving.

He went to get the horses before she had finished.

They thanked the Imam profusely for his hospitality.

The Duke left on the table a large sum of money "for those who worshipped in the Mosque."

Then once again they were on their way.

They rode fast, but Mimosa thought it was a long time before they saw once again the Aqueduct.

Then she knew they would soon be in Tunis.

It was, in fact, not yet five o'clock in the afternoon when they climbed the steep hill to Sidi Bou Said and reached the Villa.

"We are back!" Mimosa said in a rapturous voice.

She and the Duke had hardly spoken a word since they had left the Imam.

"You must go and rest," he answered.

It was the one thing she wanted to do.

She dreaded the idea of having to explain to Suzette where they had been and what had happened.

As they entered the house, Jacques gave an exclamation of delight.

A moment later Jenkins came hurrying down the stairs.

"We didn't expect Your Grace back so soon!" he said.

"The reason for that you will hear later," the Duke replied. "Miss Tison is very tired and needs to rest immediately."

"Of course," Jenkins agreed.

He ran ahead of her as Mimosa climbed very slowly up the stairs.

She expected to hear Suzette's voice at any moment.

However, when the *femme-de-chambre* came to help her undress, she said:

"I'm afraid, *M'mselle,* there is bad news of *Madame* Blanc."

"Bad news?" Mimosa questioned.

"She was so ill yesterday that we sent for the Doctor. He said it was not migraine from which she was suffering, but a fever!''

Mimosa looked at the maid in surprise, and she went on:

"They took her away to the Hospital, where she will have the proper treatment."

"I am sorry, very sorry," Mimosa managed to say.

Truthfully, of course, she was very relieved.

She would not now have to talk to Suzette and tell her all that had happened, when all she wanted to do was to rest.

She slept for three hours.

When she awoke, feeling very much better, she rang the bell.

"I have been asleep," she said unnecessarily when the *femme-de-chambre* appeared.

"*Monsieur le Duc* said we were to leave you to rest," the maid replied. "He's ordered dinner for nine o'clock and hopes you'll join him, if you feel well enough."

Mimosa jumped out of bed.

"I feel perfectly well," she said, "but I would like a bath."

This would have caused a commotion in an ordinary French household.

However, *Comte* André had been very concerned for his own comfort.

He had had installed a bathroom next to the room in which Mimosa was sleeping.

Cold water came from a tap which Mimosa was aware was very up-to-date.

The hot water had to be carried up the stairs.

After a bath scented with flowers, she put on one of the prettiest evening gowns in the wardrobe.

When she went downstairs her eyes were shining with excitement.

She was longing to see the Duke again and to talk to him.

She was only terribly afraid that he would vanish as speedily as he could after such an uncomfortable experience.

He was waiting for her in the room which looked out over the garden, wearing his evening-clothes.

As she came into the room and stood just inside the door for a few seconds, neither of them spoke.

Then he asked in a deep voice:

"You are better?"

"Yes, thank you," Mimosa replied. "I feel much better after a good sleep."

"That is what I want to hear," he said as he smiled. "There is a glass of champagne waiting for us to celebrate our return, and it is entirely thanks to you that we are both safe and unhurt."

"It will make a fascinating story to include in your book," Mimosa said, "and I only hope you collected enough material before we were so rudely interrupted."

The Duke was pouring out the champagne.

He handed a glass to her, then he raised his own.

"To a very wonderful young woman!" he said.

They drank, and as they did so, Jacques announced that dinner was ready.

The Chef, considering he had not expected them back so soon, excelled himself.

Or, perhaps, Mimosa thought, it seemed so because she was with the Duke.

Every mouthful tasted like ambrosia and every sip of wine like nectar.

Because both Jenkins and Jacques were in the Dining-Room, they did not talk of the kidnapping, but only of Thuburbo Maius.

They discussed what else might be discovered when the site was fully excavated.

They then returned to the Sitting-Room.

The lamps had been lit but the windows were open into the garden.

Outside, the stars were like diamonds in the sky.

The moon, which had guided them to safety the night before, was casting its silver light on the sea.

Mimosa went to the window.

As she felt the Duke come up behind her, she asked:

''What are . . . you going . . . to do . . . now?''

It was a question that had been hovering on her lips all evening.

She knew if he said he was leaving almost immediately she would want to cry.

Because she was afraid of revealing her feelings, she clenched the fingers of her hands.

She was trying by every means to force herself to appear controlled.

''I will answer that question later,'' the Duke said after a slight pause, ''but first I have some questions to ask you.''

Mimosa instantly felt apprehensive.

''What . . . questions?'' she enquired.

"First of all," the duke said, "how is it possible that you have such a wide knowledge of Roman Ruins?"

Mimosa did not answer, and he went on:

"Also, living, as you said you did, between America and England, how can you be so perfect in Arabic?"

Mimosa groped for an answer, but could not find one.

The Duke drew a little nearer to her.

Then he said:

"If you will not answer those questions, will you tell me how many men have kissed you before I did so yesterday?"

The question came as such a surprise that Mimosa started.

Instinctively she told the truth.

"No-one . . . no-one has . . . kissed me," she whispered, "except . . . you."

The Duke reached out his arms and turned her slowly round to face him.

"That is what I thought when I kissed you," he said. "So perhaps now you will explain to me why you are here, masquerading as Miss Minerva Tison!"

He spoke slowly, his hands holding Mimosa by the shoulders so that she could not escape from him.

She glanced up at him, then quickly away again before she said almost incoherently:

"Why . . . do you . . . ask me such a thing? It is a . . . question I . . . cannot answer!"

"Why not?" the Duke demanded.

Because she could not think what to say, Mimosa murmured:

"I . . . I think I should . . . go to bed."

She tried to move away, but the Duke's hands still held her.

"I want an answer," he said, "and it is very important."

"Why should it . . . be important?" Mimosa asked. "You have . . . seen Thuburbo Maius, which is . . . what you came . . . to see. What . . . more can . . . you want?"

"I want you!" the Duke said very quietly.

She was so astonished that her eyes opened wide and she looked up at him.

Then it was impossible to look away.

"I love you!" the Duke said softly. "I want you to be my wife."

He spoke the words with a sincerity which could not be misunderstood.

Mimosa stared at him as if she could not believe what she was hearing.

Then her whole face was transformed with a radiance which the Duke thought was not of this world.

He had never imagined that any woman could look so beautiful, so spiritual, so worshipful.

Then, as Mimosa realised what his words involved, the radiance vanished and she whispered:

"No . . . no! I cannot . . . marry you!"

"Why not? Why are you refusing me?" the Duke asked.

Because she could not escape from him, Mimosa

moved forward to hide her face against his shoulder.

His arms tightened.

In a voice he could hardly hear, she said:

"I love you . . . but I have . . . lied to . . . you."

"I thought perhaps you had."

"I could not . . . help it . . . there was nothing else I . . . c-could do."

The Duke kissed her hair before he said:

"Tell me why you lied."

"I . . . I am not . . . Minerva Tison . . ."

"I guessed that," the Duke interrupted. "In fact, I think that you are the daughter of Sir Richard Shenson."

Mimosa was so surprised that she raised her head to look up at him.

"W-why do you think . . . that?" she asked.

"When you knew how you could save us from the kidnappers," the Duke replied, "you said: 'Papa told me there are steps which would lead up onto the platform.' "

Mimosa drew in her breath.

"So . . . that was how you . . . knew who . . . I was!"

She hid her face once again against his shoulder.

"I was already bewildered and extremely curious," the Duke said, "because you seemed so pure and innocent that I could not believe any actress would play a part so skilfully."

As he spoke, the Duke put his fingers under Mimosa's chin and turned her face up to his.

"When I kissed you," he said softly, "I was quite certain you had never been kissed before."

His lips came down on hers.

Just as she had in the chamber, Mimosa felt an ecstasy streak through her.

It was as if a rapture beyond words swept her up amongst the stars.

The Duke kissed her until they were both flying in the sky.

The stars were not only overhead, but in Mimosa's breast.

It was a long time later before the Duke said:

"I love you, and although you may not believe it, I swear to you, my darling, that is something I have never said to any other woman."

There was a slight touch of mockery in his voice as he added:

"And I have never asked anybody else to marry me."

"I . . . love you . . . I love . . . you," Mimosa whispered, "but how can you . . . want to marry me . . . when I have been so deceitful?"

"You have not yet told me why you pretended to be Miss Tison," the Duke said.

"She was my Cousin . . . and when I suddenly . . . found after Papa died . . . that I had no money . . . not a penny . . . left in the Bank . . . I knew she was the . . . only person . . . if I could find her . . . who would . . . help me."

"You did not at that moment know she was in Tunis?" the Duke asked perceptively.

Mimosa shook her head.

"I had no idea of it until I read in the newspaper that she had been . . . kidnapped, but that there had been . . . no demand made for . . . a ransom as the Police had expected . . . there would be.''

Now the Duke understood why he had been told that Miss Tison had arrived home having apparently lost her memory.

"Because we . . . were so . . . alike,'' Mimosa was saying, "no-one . . . questioned that . . . I was not . . . Minerva. Then when I learned about . . . *Comte* André I was . . . shocked and . . . upset at the way . . . she had . . . behaved.''

The Duke's arms tightened as he said:

"The *Comte* is a very attractive man, and it is difficult for any woman to resist him. I can quite understand that your Cousin, having lost her Father and Mother so tragically, depended on him, and quite naturally fell in love.''

"You understand . . . you really . . . do understand!'' Mimosa said. "I thought no-one . . . ever would . . . but then . . . you are . . . different.''

"I hope so,'' the Duke said. "And now, my lovely one, you have to make people accept you as yourself, and we must forget that you ever came here pretending to be your Cousin.''

As he spoke, he thought that, unless he was mistaken, there was only *Madame* Blanc, who was in Hospital, the servants, and the Police who had interrogated her.

He thought it would be quite easy to convince them that she after all was not Minerva.

She had in fact lost her memory, but it was owing to the shock of losing her Father so suddenly.

She could revert to being herself again without too much difficulty.

Then he said:

"It may seem a strange question to ask you, my darling, but—what is your real name?"

Mimosa laughed.

"Is it really . . . true that you do . . . not know it?"

"How can I?" he asked. "I am only aware you are the daughter of a very clever man, whose book we will publish as soon as we return to England."

"Would you . . . really do that . . . for Papa?" Mimosa asked.

"Of course I will!" the Duke promised. "But I would still like to know the name of his daughter."

"It is . . . Mimosa."

"Your name is as beautiful as you are!" the Duke said.

He kissed her again until it was impossible for her to think of anything but the wonder of the wild sensations the kisses created within her.

Then the Duke said:

"I must send you to bed, my darling."

"I . . . I do not want to . . . leave you," Mimosa whispered.

"And I have no wish for you to leave me," the Duke said in a deep voice. "Never again, my beautiful one, will I sleep beside you as I did last night without touching you."

He gazed at her with love in his eyes, before he continued:

"I therefore suggest we are married as quickly as

possible and enjoy a honeymoon before we return to England.''

Mimosa looked up at him in wonder.

"Can we . . . really do that?" she asked.

"It is what we are going to do, but I think it is a mistake after what has happened to stay any longer in Tunisia. There are many other places we can visit and the most comfortable way in which to do so would be for me to hire a yacht. Then there will be no problems as to where we stay the night.''

Mimosa gave a little cry of delight.

"I would love that . . . I would love it!" she cried. "But . . . I would be happy . . . anywhere with . . . you.''

"I have never before known any woman who could say that and make me believe she is telling the truth,'' the Duke said. "You slept alone in your tent without complaint, and you also slept very peacefully on the Imam's divan!''

Mimosa chuckled.

"I do not remember anything about that! When I realised this morning that you had slept beside me . . . I felt . . . shy.''

"I adore you when you are shy,'' the Duke said, "and I have never seen anyone look as beautiful as you do when you blush.''

Mimosa blushed and hid her face against his shoulder.

"I have just thought,'' the Duke said, "that I have not asked you who your Mother was. I know now she was the sister of Clint Tison's wife. I assumed she was American.''

"Oh, no!" Mimosa answered. "She and Mama were the daughters of the Earl of Cromefield. He tried to arrange marriages for them, and never spoke to them again after they ran away with the man they loved."

The Duke stared at her.

"Cromefield!" he exclaimed. "I know the present Earl. In fact, he is a distant relative of my Mother's."

As he spoke, he thought that his relatives would be delighted he was marrying Mimosa.

It did not matter to him who she was because he loved her.

But it would make things easier for her and for her position at Court if it were known that her blood was as blue as his.

His arms tightened round Mimosa, and he told himself she was perfect in every possible way.

"Supposing," she said in a small voice, "you . . . find me very . . . dull after all the . . . exciting . . . sophisticated women you have . . . known in London and Paris."

Thoughts of Lady Sybil and *La Belle* passed briefly through the Duke's mind.

He knew they were now of no importance to him.

In a short while he would be unable to remember what they looked like.

He was aware that Mimosa was so utterly different.

She would want to take part in his adventures in Archaeology.

She would know that this was a very important part of his life.

She would grace his great house in the country, and the others he owned in London and other parts of England.

She would be completely adaptable not only because she was intelligent, but also because she loved him.

Her love was different from anything he had ever known before because for the moment it was entirely spiritual.

He would teach her the physical joys of their love.

He was quite certain that just as he was the first and only man to kiss her, he would be the last.

She would remain his in the years to come and for ever.

He drew her a little closer as if to make sure she was his and no-one could take her away from him.

Then he said:

"I will make all the arrangements for us to be married tomorrow or the next day very quietly. Then we will find exactly the right yacht to hire. We will leave the Villa and set out to explore not only new places in the Mediterranean, but also ourselves."

Mimosa gave a little gasp of joy.

Then she said:

"You . . . you have . . . forgiven me for . . . lying to you . . . and for . . . pretending to be . . . my Cousin? If she had been alive . . . I know she would have . . . helped me . . . and we would have been happy together . . . as we were when we were children."

"I will do everything I can to find out what has happened to her," the Duke promised, "but I think you must prepare yourself for the worst. I suspect she was killed trying to escape just as those criminals might have killed us."

"And . . . *Monsieur* Charlot!" Mimosa murmured.

"You said he was blackmailing you," the Duke reminded her.

"He came here . . . believing me to be Minerva," Mimosa explained. "He said he had . . . some letters which he would show to the *Comte*'s wife unless I paid him fifty thousand francs!"

"Well, I shot him," the Duke said, "and I have already notified the Police of his death. They told me they had been suspicious for some time that he was blackmailing and kidnapping people in this country, but they could not catch him in the act of doing so."

"He was an . . . evil man," Mimosa murmured.

"Then let us pray we meet no more like him, my darling. But if we do get into a tight spot, you will save me again as you saved me in Thuburbo Maius."

"You must be very . . . very careful," Mimosa warned, "because I . . . cannot lose . . . you."

"You will never do that," the Duke answered. "It is my belief, my precious, that we have been together before in other lives, and now that we have found each other in this, the Gods will be kind to us."

He gave a sigh before he went on:

"I know now that you are what I have been looking for all my life and thought I would never find."

"And I was praying," Mimosa murmured, "that I would find somebody I could love as Mama loved Papa and be as happy as they were."

"That is what we will be!" the Duke said firmly.

Then he was kissing her again, kissing her until the stars seemed to merge with the sea.

The moon enveloped them with its silver light that appeared to come from Heaven and was the Light of the Gods.

As the Duke drew Mimosa closer and closer still to him, he was saying a prayer of thankfulness because he had found what all men seek.

It was the perfection of love, a love that was unspoilt, pure, and true.

It was the love that is part of the Divine.

ABOUT THE AUTHOR

Barbara Cartland, the world's most famous romantic novelist, who is also a historian, playwright, lecturer, political speaker and television personality, has now written 618 books and sold over six hundred and twenty million copies all over the world.

She has also had many historical works published and has written four autobiographies as well as the biographies of her mother and that of her brother, Ronald Cartland, who was the first Member of Parliament to be killed in the last war. This book has a preface by Sir Winston Churchill and has been republished with an introduction by Sir Arthur Bryant.

Love at the Helm, a novel written with the help and inspiration of the late Earl Mountbatten of

Burma, Great Uncle of His Royal Highness, The Prince of Wales, is being sold for the Mountbatten Memorial Trust.

She has broken the world record for the last twenty-one years by writing an average of twenty-three books a year. In the *Guinness Book of World Records* she is listed as the world's top-selling author.

Miss Cartland in 1987 sang an Album of Love Songs with the Royal Philharmonic Orchestra.

In private life Barbara Cartland, who is a Dame of the Order of St. John of Jerusalem and Chairman of the St. John Council in Hertfordshire, has fought for better conditions and salaries for Midwives and Nurses.

She championed the cause for the Elderly in 1956, invoking a Government Enquiry into the "Housing Condition of Old People."

In 1962 she had the Law of England changed so that Local Authorities had to provide camps for their own Gypsies. This has meant that since then thousands and thousands of Gypsy children have been able to go to School, which they had never been able to do in the past, as their caravans were moved every twenty-four hours by the Police.

There are now fifteen camps in Hertfordshire and Barbara Cartland has her own Romany Gypsy Camp called "Barbaraville" by the Gypsies.

Her designs "Decorating with Love" are being sold all over the U.S.A. and the National Home Fashions League made her, in 1981, "Woman of Achievement."

She is unique in that she was one and two in the Dalton list of Best Sellers, and one week had four books in the top twenty.

Barbara Cartland's book *Getting Older, Growing Younger* has been published in Great Britain and the U.S.A. and her fifth cookery book, *The Romance of Food*, is now being used by the House of Commons.

In 1984 she received at Kennedy Airport America's Bishop Wright Air Industry Award for her contribution to the development of aviation. In 1931 she and two R.A.F. Officers thought of, and carried, the first aeroplane-towed glider airmail.

During the War she was Chief Lady Welfare Officer in Bedfordshire, looking after 20,000 Servicemen and -women. She thought of having a pool of Wedding Dresses at the War Office so a Service Bride could hire a gown for the day.

She bought 1,000 gowns without coupons for the A.T.S., the W.A.A.F.s and the W.R.E.N.S. In 1945 Barbara Cartland received the Certificate of Merit from Eastern Command.

In 1964 Barbara Cartland founded the National Association for Health of which she is the President, as a front for all the Health Stores and for any product made as alternative medicine.

This is now a £65 million turnover a year, with one-third going in export.

In January 1968 she received *La Médeille de Vermeil de la Ville de Paris*. This is the highest award to be given in France by the City of Paris.

She has sold 30 million books in France.

In March 1988 Barbara Cartland was asked by the Indian Government to open their Health Resort outside Delhi. This is almost the largest Health Resort in the world.

Barbara Cartland was received with great enthusiasm by her fans, who feted her at a reception in the City, and she received the gift of an embossed plate from the Government.

Barbara Cartland was made a Dame of the Order of the British Empire in the 1991 New Year's Honours List by Her Majesty, The Queen, for her contribution to Literature and also for her years of work for the community.

Dame Barbara has now written 618 books, the greatest number by a British author, passing the 564 books written by John Creasey.

AWARDS

1945   Received Certificate of Merit, Eastern Command, for being Welfare Officer to 5,000 troops in Bedfordshire.

1953   Made a Commander of the Order of St. John of Jerusalem. Invested by H.R.H. The Duke of Gloucester at Buckingham Palace.

1972   Invested as Dame of Grace of the Order of St. John in London by The Lord Prior, Lord Cacia.

1981   Received "Achiever of the Year" from the National Home Furnishing Association in Colorado Springs, U.S.A., for her designs for wallpaper and fabrics.

1984   Received Bishop Wright Air Industry Award at Kennedy Airport, for inventing the aeroplane-towed Glider.

1988   Received from Monsieur Chirac, The Prime Minister, The Gold Medal of the City of Paris, at the Hotel de la Ville, Paris, for selling 25 million books and giving a lot of employment.

1991   Invested as Dame of the Order of The British Empire, by H.M. The Queen at Buckingham Palace for her contribution to Literature.